The Adventures of Bove Sandle

Visions of Redemption

By Jon H. Costales

Enjoy!

Jon H. Costales

This book is dedicated to my wonderful wife Denise who supports and encourages me to do better.

Part One
First Encounters

One

Bove Sandle watched from the observation deck as the Starship Mars slid into a standard orbit around the Delta planet of Phoenix-Gamma. The trip had been quick—just under three weeks. *Too damn quick*, Bove thought. He had just finished a First Encounter assignment at Bellatrix-Pi Gamma, his fourth in a row, and was scheduled for a little R&R. Thinking of a break from the constant alertness, the constant awareness, the readiness; even in his sleep, he had to identify every little noise, every movement, every presence. The thought of a break from that is what kept him going.

Phoenix-Gamma was a magnitude three star sixty degrees south of the solar equator and twenty-four light-years from Earth. The Delta planet was considered an ideal site for the next colony and this assignment was a last-minute decision that needed immediate attention. Bove had been assigned to the team on his last day on Pi-3. He complained but was told that leave time was up to the discretion of the task controller, and if he didn't agree with the department's policy, he could file a complaint and proceed through proper channels. He complained again but to no avail.

He had joined the Galactic Peacekeeper Force, the GPF, five years ago when a global Manifest Destiny had been announced. Man was now ready to move to the stars, and Bove had wanted to be part of it. His standard training was two years of intensive instruction covering piloting of every known starship made, from small private pleasure craft to large warships of battle class. Every hand-held weapon available was covered in the smallest detail so Bove was able to assemble and disassemble each one in the dark. In addition to learning weapons, they were trained in fighting techniques—formal combat to hand-to-hand encounters covering techniques of karate, tae-kwon-do, jujitsu, and street fighting. Survival was covered in three months and included the harshest environments starting in the desert, moving to mountains, then jungles and forests, and culminating in the arctic snow where winter temperatures dropped to sixty degrees below zero Fahrenheit.

They were prepared for almost any situation they could find themselves in. Able to protect themselves with any weapon available or with only their bare hands, and escape in any available ship. They were the best. Once their training was complete, they had earned a two-week break, after which Bove received his first assignment--the excitement ran high--the adventure had begun.

Now, as then, his assignment read, *Possible intelligent life has been identified...*, and went on in more detail to explain; but, as usual, it came down to checking out possible colony sites.

Most intelligent life they had found was on such a low level that future development was unlikely--or so the Peacekeepers deemed.

The great adventure had developed into a job. Seldom was there any adventure, it had become a routine. Once the First Encounter Teams reached their designated sites, they checked for intelligent life, did their tests--soil, water, plants, animals, weather, seasons, etc.--and then wrote it up. The report was considered along with various other tabulations of data in selecting the next colonization move in the great plan. Once the data was assembled it would take a majority of negative reports to change the decision whether it was to colonize or not. The Peacekeepers made sure the desired recommendation was clearly understood before any teams were dispatched—just to avoid any disagreement in the filed reports. No one wanted to explain to their superiors why an expectation was not met. Particularly if the planet had been flagged as an ideal site for a colony, which was the case with the Delta planet of Phoenix-Gamma.

Bove did not know why he stayed with the Peacekeepers, but right now he only wanted a break. For the first time in eighteen months, he had thought of letting the tension slip away only to have that hope dashed when this assignment came through. He took a deep breath and studied the blue orb of the Delta planet arcing across the observation window--a peaceful welcoming haven. The Mars was heading to the night side of the planet where a dark line divided day from night. It seemed to pull at him, to bring him down onto its surface and into the forest of trees towering above him, great brown giants brooding over him. Then he was there among the tree-tops and with him were others like him. They lived here in the trees in a village built high in the branches hidden from the ground below and the sky above. And he knew this was their world. They were there for him, to support him, to guide him in his decisions--to help him make the right decision. He could feel their love and their confidence in him, sure he would be there for them. Then they were gone, and he was back on the observation deck looking at the calm blue planet. *Strange*, he thought blinking his eyes. *What just happened? Did I pass out? Fall asleep? I felt like I was standing in the forest among the trees.*

"Surface team report to briefing room C." The voice cut into his thoughts, "...briefing room C." It took the repeat for him to realize it affected him. He turned from the window and yearned to turn back but could not. He closed out those thoughts and instead opened his eyes to the world, sharpened his ears, and toned his awareness. He felt a ripple of security at this heightened sensual perception but yearned for the serenity of relief.

"Too damn quick," he muttered and headed through the exit to the transport tube. Seconds later he stepped out of the tube, and headed down the hall, to briefing room C. The room contained seven rows of ten seats. In the front was a table with a whiteboard hanging on the wall behind it. Five Agents sat scattered around the room—none of which Bove knew. Bove paused just inside the door looked around, and then settled into an empty chair at the back of the room.

Commander Kramer entered at the front and stepped up to the table just as Bove settled in his seat. Kramer was a tall man with short-cropped hair graying at the temples. He wore a tan uniform shirt and matching pants, both newly pressed and crisp. He had no notes and placed his hands behind his back as he glanced around the room. "This is a special situation," he said. "On Gamma-4 we have discovered three sites with ancient ruins constructed by intelligent life. They're thousands of years old and have been uninhabited for almost that long. The ruins reflect an intelligent life form, but there seems to be no further development." Kramer glanced around the room.

Bove shifted, as did a couple of others.

"Because of this," Kramer continued, "we believe whoever built those ruins has long since died. There are no other ruins on the planet and probably no intelligent life. If there is, we will deal with them later. This mission will concentrate on the ruins and what they contain." Kramer paused glanced around the room and then continued before anyone could voice a concern, "We want to use the First Encounter Team because of your experience with alien cultures. You'll know the meaning of their symbols, you'll understand their beliefs, their reasoning, and hopefully their destiny. Your exposure to alien cultures and symbols will be invaluable."

The agent seated in front and to the right of Bove shifted, then raised his hand head high. "What should we do if there is intelligent life?"

"This mission is limited to investigating the ruins only, Dickens," Kramer replied. "You will do your normal environment tests to determine if the planet will physically support us and report on your findings concerning the ruins. Is that clear?"

Again, the room shifted, and glances darted about. It did not feel right to Bove, not right at all. Why was the First Encounter Team put in if they were not going to encounter? And why are they not to report contact? Political? Economical? Gamma-4 was very Earth-like, slightly warmer though making it like a paradise--very desirable for a colony. And it was the first suitable planet they had found in Sector II which was critical to the success of the Manifest.

"You'll go down in teams of two," Kramer continued. "Each team will study a single predetermined site for ten days. When you return to the Mars and file your reports, you'll be free to continue with whatever you were planning." Again, he paused for a moment, then continued. "You have your orders. I know you've encountered this before, but each time is new. We don't know what's down there, so I want you to be aware and be careful, I don't want any surprises."

"Sir," Dickens said. "Who found the ruins? I mean, what do we know about them?"

Kramer looked at Dickens, then glanced around the room. "Report to shuttle bay three for departure in fifteen minutes," he said then turned and left.

Bove looked around the room, *something's wrong*, he thought, *we're not here to encounter, and we're not to report encounters?* Sure, he did not have all the facts, but it looked to him like a clear-cut case of pushing aside the natives and taking their planet. Yet that was not what the manifest was about, or so he had been told.

Two

The shuttle bay was on the underside of the starship facing Gamma-4, and at perigee, they could land within an hour. Optimum departure was twenty minutes away when the Mars made its closest approach to the surface.

Bove stood next to the shuttle that rose four meters high. He held his helmet under his arm, the only piece of his suit not on him. Standard procedure was to suit up before entering the shuttle bay where a single mistake could void the bay of air. If that were to happen everything not secured would be forced out the bay door along with all the air. So, being fully suited was a requirement before entering the shuttle bay. But, as had become standard practice, the agents held their helmets tightly under their arms, since there had never been an error that voided the bay.

Bove, being the pilot, was responsible for checking the shuttle's integrity before every flight. He circled the shuttle checking for flaws in the hull, verifying the landing pads were clean and well-oiled, that engine shields were solid, that the cockpit window was clear of pockmarks, and that all doors were sealed tightly. Everything looked good, and he noted how close it resembled every other shuttle he had flown.

One of the nice things about the Manifest was the standardization it had created. Every starship, military or commercial, was made with standard components from the engines to the control consoles on the bridge. The external shell could be any form or style the manufacturer wanted which allowed the internal configuration to be individualized to the consumer's needs. They may all look different, but they all flew alike.

This shuttle, like most in the fleet, had room for six including the pilot and navigator. Behind the crew compartment was the cargo bay. There was a rear door that lowered to create a ramp for loading and unloading cargo. Open on the side facing Bove was the crew entrance that had a set of steps and an arched upper section allowing easy access for the crew.

Bove turned when he heard someone approach. His partner, he assumed, stopped next to him. He was about the same height with dark hair and brown eyes that studied Bove's face.

"Steps?" Bove asked, reading his nameplate.

"Yeah, Jonathan Steps."

"Bove Sandle. How long you been in?"

"Three years, you?"

"Five," Bove turned back to the shuttle for a final look.

Bove had never been paired with the same person in all his missions. It was a standard rule of the GPF that no two agents were to be assigned together more than once. They said it was to avoid attachments that could cause mental stress.

Particularly if something happened to one agent. Because of that rule, Bove had no real friends in the GPF and none outside the job.

"How does it look?" Steps asked.

Bove nodded, "Fine, you see anything?"

Steps shook his head. The navigator was responsible for checking the cargo on every flight, and Steps confirmed that the cargo was as it should be. "Everything's standard. Normal mission previsions." He said then added, "Doesn't feel normal though."

Bove just looked at him knowing what he meant and feeling the same. He did not acknowledge the comment. "Let's do this." He climbed the steps and went forward to the pilot's seat. Steps followed and settled into the navigator's seat next to him. Both put their helmets over their heads and secured them with the locking ring around the neck.

Bove checked his communications link verifying it was set to internal. "All clear," he said, "beginning the hatch sealing procedure." He turned on the internal air, then reached down and pressed a button on the left side of his control panel. The hatch closed and sealed with a quiet hiss. He punched a few buttons turning on all the systems and watched lights flash across the control panel. As each system completed its self-test the lights settled into a soft green glow.

"Everything okay, Steps?"

"Everything's a *go*. We're ready."

"Okay," Bove switched his radio channel to the landing bay control room. "Shuttle Two verified and ready for exit," he said.

"Stand by," the control room voice responded.

"Standing by," Bove answered. *Let's get this show on the road*, he thought. Ten days and he would be headed for a long rest. Maybe he would try one of the systems in Pisces, he had heard they were good for the soul--and other parts. Then a voice cut into his thoughts. *You must believe, watch, listen, and believe.*

"Huh," Bove said. *What was that?* It felt like someone was there in the shuttle with them. He glanced back over his shoulder then toward Steps who started to say something then turned back to the control panel. There could not be anyone in the shuttle with them, Steps had checked the cargo bay and found it filled with their equipment for the mission. The crew section had only six seats and no place where someone could hide. No, there could not be anyone in the shuttle with them. So, what had he heard?

"Landing team," the control room voice said. "Stand by for shuttle bay door opening."

It took a second for Bove to realize what was said. He forced his thoughts back to reality, then turned on his forward screen to watch the shuttle bay door slide open. Shuttle One rose from the deck, glided out the opening, and turned out of sight.

"Shuttle Two cleared for exit," the voice said.

Bove powered up the thruster engine, released the gravity lock, and felt the pull of the restraining straps against his chest as he throttled up the engine. The shuttle glided toward the open door and the serene blue orb beyond.

They burst away from the Mars with increasing velocity and then tilted up to fly parallel to the planet's surface. A soft beep alerted Bove that they had cleared the Mars, and to activate the auto-pilot system. He did. The shuttle adjusted its angle of descent until it was speeding ahead of the Mars in a lower orbit on a trajectory to the far side of the planet.

Three

Forty minutes later yellow lights flashed across the control panel indicating the auto-landing sequence had initiated. Bove punched several buttons on the right side of the main screen to verify that the auto-landing was set and to display the landing site. A full-color topographical picture appeared; underneath was coded information about the map. Colors showed thick vegetation and open spreads of grass. *Jungle*, Bove thought, *with areas of grassland*. A red line traced their planned path over the jungle, into a looping turn, and down into a long green valley. Three kilometers south of their landing site were the ruins nestled in the jungle and indicated in blue on the display.

The main thruster light turned yellow. "Landing sequence started," Bove announced.

"Confirmed," Steps answered.

Maneuvering jets fired flipping the shuttle over so its underside was facing the atmosphere. The main thruster fired slowing the craft enough to cause it to drop out of orbit. Pressure pushed against Bove's chest making it hard to breathe.

They hit the atmosphere increasing the pressure. Then as the shuttle slowed the pressure eased until their velocity was reduced enough to activate the maneuvering jets allowing Bove to take control. He left the autopilot on and studied the main viewer. The display showed the approach, at first it was clouds and heatwaves, but then it cleared. The sea was beneath them, and ahead was a vast forest covering the land in waves of green. When they crossed the coast, their altitude was too high to distinguish the individual trees, but after traveling a hundred kilometers inland details became clear. It was then that Bove realized the trees towered over three hundred meters in height.

He took a deep breath, glad for the release of pressure, and studied the mountains, hills, rivers, and lakes, then the long green clearing of their destination. The autopilot brought the shuttle lower until they were at the treetops and when they reached the clearing the shuttle stopped its forward motion and hovered for a moment, then dropped into the clearing. It paused ten meters above the green meadow, then slid to the right over a level spot, and settled to the ground.

Bove checked all the systems, powered down the main thrusters, and then switched to standby. While he verified that the atmosphere was acceptable to breathe Steps checked the area for several kilometers around to identify any threat. The air was satisfactory, and no threat was found.

Bove snapped open the securing ring on his helmet, lifted it over his head, then, opened the hatch which gave a hiss and a pop. Cool fresh air drifted into the shuttle, and after a couple of minutes, it reached the cockpit replacing the stale air from the Mars. Bove and Steps inhaled the freshness with three or four self-satisfying breaths.

"Nice," Steps spread his arms sucking in more fresh air.

"Yeah, it is. Let's get out of here and see what we've got." Bove made a final systems check, then got up and headed for the shuttle exit. It was early morning with the sun shining brightly over the treetops, and the cool air was refreshing on his face. It was a welcome change from the artificial atmosphere of the Mars.

Steps came out behind Bove and stopped. They stood looking at the landing site while the environment filled them with awe and energy. Birds hidden high in the trees chirped their happy songs, and the trees stood in quiet tribute to the strangers below.

The clearing was three hundred by five hundred meters of vibrant green grass bordered by a forest of giant trees. They were the trees that Bove saw while on the observation deck of the Mars, but from a different point of view. Their dark gnarled bark covered the enormous trunks and high above massive branches intertwined, broad six-pointed leaves spread out like giant hands creating a dense canape that blocked most of the sunlight making the forest dark and forbidding. A stark contrast to the bright sunlight streaming across the meadow, and unlike the forest Bove had seen in his dream.

He felt a slight shiver run across his shoulders and down his back like a warning, yet he was drawn toward the trees by a mysterious power quelling his apprehension with a calm assurance of safety. He shook and took a deep breath calming his nerves, then looked again at the forest. He pulled away, turned, and looked at Steps. The vague feeling of being watched twitched his skin, then it was gone. "Let's get set up," he said and opened the cargo bay.

They worked for the rest of the day, first setting up their camp—a tent with plenty of room to review data, fix meals, store supplies, and sleep two. Once that was completed, they spent the rest of the day setting up equipment at various locations around the clearing. A security perimeter that circled the camp was the first item to establish. Then monitors to check weather, temperature, air pressure, humidity, wind patterns, rainfall, and storm indicators. Land status, earthquakes, volcanoes, and general shifting of landmasses. Air quality, CO_2 levels, ozone in the upper atmosphere, oxygen levels, and nitrogen levels. It took the rest of that day and the next morning to assemble their monitors, calibrate them, and place them where they could gather the most information. When they had finished the sun was high in the sky.

"The ruins are about three kilometers south of here," Bove said. "We should check them out." He gazed into the forest and again he felt a shiver as if someone were watching. He shook it off.

They boarded the shuttle, sealed the hatch, and after completing the system check Bove fired up the main engines. The shuttle rose straight up until it was level with the treetops then he turned to the south toward the ruins.

They hovered over the remains of a small

town scanning the ground with penetrating sensors to determine the extent of the site. All data were recorded in the shuttle's main storage unit along with displaying it on the monitors for review.

"Not much here," Steps said. "Looks like the town center is all that's left."

"Yeah," Bove agreed. "Houses seem to have surrounded the main town."

The sensors showed the remains of several buildings buried around the town. The few buildings that still were visible above ground were made of stone with gaping holes where doors and windows used to be. The largest structure had three stories above ground and appeared to have five more buried. Several others had multiple stories above and below ground level.

Bove lowered the shuttle to the ground where the homes of the residents of this small town once stood. What had become of the people that once lived here was the main question on Bove's mind. There was no indication of a major disaster of any kind, so the question remained.

They disembarked, shouldered their equipment, and headed to the closest building. After searching through several of the secondary buildings and finding nothing but empty rooms and blocked stairwells, they decided to head back to camp. Bove stopped before going into the shuttle to study the remaining building, there was nothing to see above ground. *...what is to be found*, he thought, *will be found below*.

"Looks like our work is cut out for us," Steps said.

"Yeah," Bove looked beyond the structure at the darkening forest. "Tomorrow," He said, "we'll see what's there."

Back at camp they made some food and settled in for the night. Steps checked the security fence they had installed around the campsite to warn them of any animals or other intruders that may decide to visit during the night; all looked secure. They settled in for a good night's sleep.

Four

Bove turned and tried to clear his head, he closed his eyes and listened to the planet. The trees were alive, and high in their branches, he could hear whispers like sounds. He could see movement, and he could feel it, the brush of a leaf then a gripping--a holding. He tried to open his eyes, but sleep had him and he could not shake off the slumber. The trees reached down with their branches encircling him with a warm cover, seducing him to surrender.

Their thick trunks, fifteen to twenty meters around, were clear of branches up to seventy meters, but above that, the branches were dense enough to hide the stars. Leaves rustled with movement in the still air. Something—someone—called to him. *You must believe.*

They were ascending to the trees. One by one the baskets rose into the high branches carrying people and supplies. Another basket lowered close by, waiting while a man, woman, and two children loaded their belongings then themselves. The basket rose disappearing into the high branches. Another followed and yet another appeared next to Bove.

He helped load the items piled close by and

watched as another couple disappeared into the canape; swallowed by the lush green blanket above. Basket after basket lowered and was filled until it became his turn. Into it he loaded all his belongings, then himself to be lifted to his new home.

Why they ascended to the trees was unknown to him, but he felt he would soon learn. They had left their village in the forest to live in the trees. The trees gave them everything they needed—food, shelter, safety. In the trees, they had rebuilt their village among the branches.

He no longer thought of the Mars, or the mission, although he knew of them. He thought of the changes they would bring. Colonization, the influx of people, the cutting of trees, and the building of shelters. And as he traveled the tree branches, he knew it was his life that would be affected, his forest, his home. *What have I become?* He wondered. It frightened him, yet he wanted it to remain.

The branches were familiar, he had traveled this route before. Intersections and special trees; he knew them all, like old friends.

He reached his village; branches were connected by planks making a vast base for the huts that were scattered through the treetops. The trees still grew around the village forming tunnels running from hut to hut. Bove knew where to go. He passed several huts and glanced into a couple that had open windows, or doors, but there was no one in sight. Finally, he arrived at the one he was to enter, he knew it was right, but he didn't know why.

It was larger than it appeared from the outside, and it had several doors leading from the entry. Again, he knew where to go, which room to enter, and in which chair to sit.

It was only after he had settled himself into a comfortable position that he noticed someone sitting opposite him. The room was dim, and details were obscured except for two eyes gazing knowingly at him, boring into him. He turned in his seat pulling away from the hypnotizing eyes and glanced around the room. His eyes adjusted to the dim light so he could make out walls made of large leaves attached to the support branches giving the hut an angular shape. His head was spinning, he had no clear memory of the person on the other side of the room, only glimpses of a peaceful welcoming haven. *What am I doing here*? he wondered, *what is this place*?

He turned towards the man sitting across from him. He was older with gray hair and a short beard, angler cheeks, and soft blue eyes that seemed to understand Bove's every thought. Bove let his eyes run over the man. He was wearing a light-flowing robe that revealed his general shape and slenderness. His arm lay over the arm of the chair and his hand hung loosely over the edge.

"I am Kabluff," he said drawing Bove's attention back. "And you are Bove."

Bove had not seen him move his mouth or any other part of himself, yet he had heard his remark – or Kabluff's remark. He waited, then thought, *this is okay*.

"Yes, it's okay," Kabluff said. He spoke by matching Bove's brain wave pattern, then transferring his thoughts. "I have brought you here so you can feel what it is like to be Krytheon and understand why you must help us. We know of the plans to colonize Kryth, and we must stop them. You and I -- together."

"Kry..." Bove started.

"Phoenix-Gamma Delta to you," Kabluff said, switching to vocal, "at least while you are among them."

Bove sat stunned for a moment, *while I am among them*… echoed through his thoughts. *This is a dream*, he assured himself, *I can wake up any time I want…*, but he could not.

"You have already felt it, and you liked it. Did you not?" Kabluff gazed into Bove's eyes, studying his every reaction.

Felt what? Bove wondered, yet he knew, and his head spun. He had enjoyed the ascent to the trees, the release from the pull of the earth below. It blended until it was one; joy and longing for the familiar, spinning in his mind. *What am I doing here?* he wondered. *This is not right*.

"We were once earthbound, like you before we became enlightened and free. Like you, we took what we wanted because it was there to be taken, but that was thousands of years ago." Kabluff said gazing at Bove unflinchingly. "Now we know better, and one day you will reach this same plain, but it takes time, and until then you must stay away." Kabluff paused, studied Bove, then continued, "Now you understand. You have seen what you are, and what we have become."

Bove shook his head, "I'm not a savage, I'm not here to take what I like."

"We both know you are here to study the ruins, then more will come and settle. Look and see what will happen if you stop them." Kabluff raised and twisted his hand, "See what you will preserve."

Bove saw the huts scattered among the treetops, not just in this area, but all over the planet. He saw the Krytheons, then there became fewer until there were none. But they were not gone, for they looked through Bove's eyes at the empty huts that were no longer needed. They had moved to another existence, another level of nonphysical existence.

His vision swept from the planet's surface to its two moons, then to its sun. He saw the entire system, spinning in the emptiness of space, and there were many systems, closer and closer together. They were moving in a galactic spin, tighter and brighter, one of many sparkling diamonds on the black velvet sky.

"Take one," Kabluff said, "a galaxy to do with as you wish, as will we. Let me show you." Suddenly an entire galaxy spun between them, and Kabluff reached out and touched a star that was starting to expand into a supernova – it calmed. "See I have just saved a planet, given them a second chance -- I have become their God."

Bove shuddered.

"If you come you will destroy us; you will destroy the future Gods of the universe. But if you stay away as others have, we will reward you. You will be special, a chosen one, and you will be treated as such.

"I can only show you what is, and what will be, you must choose the path we are to travel." Kabluff closed his eyes for an instant, then looked again into Bove's eyes.

This is a dream, Bove assured himself and looked back at Kabluff. His seat was soft yet firm and comfortable, the musty scent of dried leaves tickled his nostrils, and his skin cooled from the soft breeze. He watched Kabluff but did not wake.

"Perhaps tomorrow we'll talk more, and of course, you can come to us any time, just come to the forest and stand among the trees." Kabluff looked again at Bove feeling his confusion, and yet Bove was comfortable with his dream. "You will learn," Kabluff said. "Go now, you must make haste, for you have work to do and reports to file."

Bove nodded and rose to leave. When he stepped from the room, he was alone on the forest floor. The trees towered above him and there was no sign of other life. He reached out to touch a nearby tree feeling its life warm against his palm.

Five

Bove turned in his sleeping bag and pushed it from him. He sat up on the side of his cot and stretched. He stood up and stepped out of the tent. The first light of day was brightening the canopy to the east. He blinked and looked at the trees, the leaves swayed with the morning breeze and the chirps of the birds played against his ears. He stepped back into the tent.

"Steps," he said. Steps in deep sleep lay on his cot not stirring.

Bove looked at his hands and flexed his fingers remembering the warmth of the trees, then rubbed the sleep from his face and head. He yawned, and smiled to himself, *bad dreams*, he thought.

"Steps," he said, louder.

"Huh," Steps mumbled.

"We have a load of stuff to do. We need to get moving."

"Yeah, right, just as soon as I wake up." Steps turned his back to Bove and shrugged under his cover.

"Well, you can catch up," Bove said. He went out of the tent to finish waking up, and by the time he was finished, Steps had gotten himself fully awake and was getting their breakfast packets out of the storage bin.

"How'd you sleep last night?" Steps asked.

"Fine, you?"

"Fine. Did you dream?" Steps handed Bove breakfast, a packet of gelatin nutrients, a wafer, and a self-heating cup of coffee. "I did. A strange dream, but I don't remember it. I was in a room, talking to someone... I don't remember. You know how dreams are."

"Yeah," Bove said, "I was in the forest alone, just looking at the trees. Just standing there looking up at the trees. They're so big." He felt a shiver run across his shoulders.

"Was that it? Just looking at trees?" Steps asked.

"Yeah..." Bove stared into the forest. It stood towering like a protective wall, yet warm and knowing. Bove shook his head and took a sip of coffee.

"What's the plan?" Steps asked chewing on a bread-like wafer, then washing it down with coffee.

"We'll check out the rest of the ruins, see what we can find."

"Good enough."

They finished eating and took the shuttle up over the forest to the ruins. Once the shuttle was down and secure, they disembarked and headed for the center building—the only one they had not explored. As they approached it, it seemed to grow larger until it towered above them like a giant stone statue embedded in the earth.

Like the smaller buildings, it was empty,

consisting of supporting pillars and fragments of dividing walls -- dust and stones covered the floor. At its center was a large stone room, still intact except for its door at the far end. In it was a stairwell, broken and crumbling but passable on the downward side. It was clear from the broken windows and walls that the upper floors offered nothing of value.

"You see any reasons to go up?" Bove asked.

"Nope."

"Me neither. We can report there was no access."

"Maybe we should go up one floor." Steps suggested.

They did and found no access farther up. Nothing but rubble on the second floor, so they turned their attention to below. They spend most of the day going deeper into the structure only to find nothing but empty rooms and broken doors. Windows that once looked out on the forest were crowded with dirt that spilled onto the floor. The air was filled with the musty smell of packed soil and roots. The building revealed nothing.

They stepped out into the late afternoon sunshine, exhausted, hungry, and disillusioned at finding nothing but emptiness. Back at their camp they fixed food and relaxed outside their tent.

Bove sat in a portable chair and gazed into the forest. Two hundred meters across the grass the trees stood like dark pillars of some lost structure; steady against the changing seasons and changing with the steady cycle of life. It pulled him, gently, easily -- seductively.

Was it a dream last night? He wondered. *It seemed so real, and I remember every detail, not like a dream.* He shifted in the chair and then stood up.

Come to the forest and stand among the trees… If I want to see them again, but he said we would talk again. Bove rubbed his hand across his face in confusion and focused on the trees. *Okay,* he decided and started toward the forest.

"Where are you going?" Steps asked, watching him walk away.

Bove paused. "I'm going to check out the forest." He continued with long strides across the grass and into the shadowed security of the trees. The clearing, and everything in it, quickly disappeared as the forest closed around him shutting out all else. He stopped among the trees watching dapples of light dance across the forest floor as the leaves above shifted in the breeze. There were movement and sounds, birds fluttering, monkeys calling through the branches, and the wind rustling the leaves. *Come to the forest, to the trees.* Bove thought again of Kabluff's comment. He stood there in the shade for a while watching, listening, and waiting. *Where are they?* He wondered looking up into the high branches. There was slight movement as the leaves shifted in the gentle breeze that rustled the forest canape. He felt tired, and sleepy, and lowered himself to the ground among the soft duff. He leaned against the trunk of one of the giant trees and closed his eyes. "You wish to speak again?"

The voice shocked Bove's eyes open. He sat up and looked around expecting to see Steps, but the forest was peaceful, calming, and void of anyone.

A dream, he thought. "I need answers," he said feeling foolish talking to trees, yet hoping for a response. None came. *So much for contact or intelligent life.* He shook his head and ran a hand through his hair. *They were only dreams*, he stood, looked around again, and headed back to their camp.

Steps had built a fire near the tent. It was early fall on Gamma-Delta, and the temperature became cool in the evenings, much like early fall on Earth. The sun had dropped behind the trees to the west, casting their small camp into shadow. Steps threw more wood on the fire, and Bove shivered.

"What did you see in the forest?" Steps sat next to him glancing over and then turned toward the fire.

"Who do you think built the town?" Bove stared into the flames.

"Whoever it was is long gone."

"I don't know. Maybe they are relocated. Moved to another part of the planet."

"We would have picked up some indication of them. Either technology or signs of a village— smoke, huts, buildings most likely. There would be some indication. They're long gone."

"Some disaster you think?"

"Yeah, probably."

"Wouldn't there be some trace of that?"

"Maybe we just haven't found it yet. A meteor could wipe out everything and leave no trace if enough time has passed. Or a large volcano could block the sunlight long enough to kill off most life. Over time the atmosphere would clear, and any trace would be quickly covered with vegetation. Kramer did say the ruins were thousands of years old."

"Yeah, I suppose you're right." Bove turned back to the fire in deep thought. *Should I tell Steps about the dreams? Can I trust him? Will he think I've lost it?*

He turned towards Steps looking him in the eye considering, then said, "We should get some sleep." *I should sleep in the forest*, Bove added to himself, *high in the treetops.*

The shadows turned into darkness, night slipped across the clearing, and sleep pushed into Bove's mind.

Six

Again, the forest pulled at him, and sleep calmed his mind. Images of dreams once dreamt slipped through the forest of his thoughts, flowing from tree to tree. He pulled his blanket around himself and settled in his cot. Soon his eyes were closed, his body relaxed, and his breathing deepened. His mind was slipping from reality into the world of dreams.

The trees reached over his head, covered the sky, and beckoned him to come to them. They reached down and enclosed him in their branches, then lifted him above the shuttle, and the clearing, and the forest. He shook his head trying to push the images away, trying to break free of the vision. Higher he went until the forest was a green blanket covering the planet with clouds obscuring parts. He saw the curvature of the planet as he moved higher.

He was on the observation deck of the Mars watching the blue orb of Gamma-4. He left to prepare his supplies for the landing on Kryth -- his new home. He was with the first batch of colonists, and they would be going down to the surface in the morning. He was nervous.

They were landing, then they were settled

next to a great stone skeleton of a building, and things were fine, but the forest frightened them. It intimidated them, and they had to push it back. Just a little at first, then a bit more, then another push.

The Krytheons responded. They beckoned the colonists to the forest, then they invaded their minds twisting and turning their thoughts. At first, the colonists could not remember why they were there. To build a colony, but they did not want to do that. Knowing they must proceed they wondered how and what was needed. They had everything to survive, so what more was required? Then they began to wonder why there were so many of them. Everything would be fine with just a few, so some had to be eliminated, and soon.

Bove took care of it.

More colonists came, and Bove watched them from the trees. They were better prepared for they had learned from before. Bove worried *it would be harder this time*. But it was not, their weapons were stronger, but their minds were the same, weak, and easily manipulated. Bove affected all, their worth was gone. Soon they all died from in-fighting. But this was not the end, they would come back as long as there were ones to come.

And they did. With bigger, stronger machines; and bigger, stronger weapons. Bove commanded a battlecruiser, and he guided it over the last of the great forests. Their enemy was trapped in a few hundred square kilometers of trees that would soon be burning.

"Activate the lasers," he commanded.

"Yes sir," snapped the response.

Bove saw the trees, then he saw the village, the huts, and the Krytheons going about their business of living. And he thought of the many men and women needlessly killed, and the many lives the Krytheons had taken.

"Fire!" he ordered.

It was done. Bove closed his eyes, but to no avail, he was there in the village. The laser blasted through the trees, ripping out trunks and searing branches. The trees split crashing to the ground and carrying the Krytheons with them. Those that were missed were left to burn. It was not over; they would be back until there were no trees and no Krytheons.

Bove shuddered and dropped a rope three hundred meters to the ground, it was the only way out. He followed the rope, but the ground was gone, as was Kryth and everything he had known.

He was sitting across from Kabluff, in the same room where he had first met him. Candles burned on the small table to his left, casting light across Kabluff's face so his features seemed to flicker in and out of reality. "Is this real?" Bove asked, then answered himself, "No, it's a dream. Isn't it?"

"You are both here and there," Kabluff told him. "You dream and I am in your dream. Yet I am real, and you are here beside me, as real as the trees in which we sit."

Bove was dazed. "You're making this up," he said. "No! You're a dream, you're not even real. You're me."

"I *am* real. It's true you dream, but you are

here as well, in a separate reality. A here and there. Just as I am here and there in both space and time. I see what has been and what will be, and I have shown you the results of your decision, or lack of one." Kabluff looked deep into Bove's eyes.

"My decision?" Bove wondered.

"Yes," Kabluff said, "you have the power."

Bove opened his mouth but was speechless.

Kabluff's blue eyes faded into the gray of morning peeking through the trees. Bove sat bold upright, throwing his blanket off, "Wait," he cried.

"What? Why?" Steps answered turning from the supply tub where he was gathering pouches for breakfast. "What's the matter with you?"

"A dream, just a dream," Bove dropped his head into his hands trying to clear his thoughts.

"Yeah." Steps grabbed two self-warming cups of coffee for Bove and himself and sat Bove's on the shelf. "Sounded more like a nightmare to me. What's going on?"

"Nothing!" Bove snapped, then took a deep breath.

"Yeah, well you tossed around last night and the night before. Are you having bad dreams?" Steps glared at him. "Is there something I need to worry about?"

"No!" Bove stood up and turned to Steps. "Forget it. I'm fine. Just tired. I'm due for a break and shouldn't be on this mission."

"Well, you are." Steps took a sip of coffee.

Bove dropped back on his cot. "Yeah, I

am." He ran a hand through his hair.

"So, are you having bad dreams?"

"Strange dreams is more like it." Bove shook his head and rubbed his face.

"Want to talk about it?"

"No, they're just dreams. They don't mean anything. I can deal with them."

"Yeah," Steps said handing Bove a breakfast pouch.

Seven

They spent the next few days mapping the rest of the ruins with ground-penetrating sensors to create a map of the entire town. In the forest, they found more subsurface ruins and a couple of structures above ground. Structures they thought had to be explored which they did and found nothing but empty rooms and broken doorways.

After nine days of mapping and exploring the ruins they decided they had enough information, although they had not found any artifacts or evidence that anyone had occupied the town. It was time to prepare to leave.

The next morning, they began to shut down all the test equipment and verify the data.

Bove reviewed the data from the sensors and the mappings of the ruins while Steps closed down the equipment and packed it into crates.

Like the memories of my dreams, Bove thought, *solid yet featureless*. The whole planet was like that, it was alive, but nothing was happening. It just was. Yet there was more than that, the forest was there, pushing at Bove as if it had a spirit yearning to be alone again. *...no intelligent life. ...we will deal with them later*. Was the forest alive and conscience? Was it trying to talk to him through the dreams? Were the Krytheons trying to tell him something?

Steps came into the tent, grabbed a bottle of water, and took a long drink. He stretched his arms and back then sat across from Bove. "What a waste to come here and find nothing," he said.

Bove looked up at him and shook his head. "Maybe there's more here than we saw." He studied Steps to see his reaction, but Steps simply shook his head.

"No," he said. "There's nothing here. We saw everything this planet has to offer including a past that's long dead."

Bove shifted in his chair and leaned back. He questioned the truth of his dream; if there were aliens that could enter your mind at will, they could go in and make the planet look uninhabitable, then the agents would be on their way. But they did not do that, instead, they let the planet's beauty be known, and its fruits tasted, and then they told me what would happen if one of two choices was made. But there are other options: why could the planet not be shared? Bove thought if he could talk to Kabluff once more, he could show him. The colonists would stay out of the forests, and the Krytheons would leave them alone, he could explain that to him.

"What's going on?" Steps cut into his thoughts.

Bove looked at him, thoughts still drifting through his mind. He closed his eyes and pinched the bridge of his nose. "Nothing's going on."

"You look perturbed." Steps poked.

"Nothing is going on." Bove looked up at

Steps, eyes fixed on him.

"Okay." Steps raised his hands, palms facing out.

Bove sat up, looked back at the terminal, and tried to focus on the data, but questions kept pushing at him. *Should I talk to him?* he wondered. Just because he noticed something did not mean that he would understand. *He may think I'm crazy. Or he may have had dreams or visions also. But he doesn't act like it. Nothing seems to be bothering him.* Bove considered his options. He could recommend no colonization, but on what grounds? Dreams? He could talk to the other agents, but would they think him crazy, and report him? Even if they listened to him would it change their minds? Doubtful.

Steps stood up. "You sure nothing's going on?"

Bove looked up but did not respond.

"Okay." Steps left.

If anyone else had a vision they would have to believe him, he considered. But when could he talk to anyone? Reports are filed first thing upon returning to the ship. Then within an hour, there will be a debrief. There will be no time to see anyone. So, that leaves Steps, and if he has had a vision would he recommend no colonization? He does not act like it.

Bove leaned back unable to concentrate on the data. He realized that if he recommended no colonization there would be a reinvestigation of the site and new reports and recommendations made. And if those did not agree with his reports, he could be put on desk duty, and that is the last thing he wanted.

Yet, if he did nothing, would he be condemning the Krytheons to extinction? And could he live with that? That was the ultimate question nagging at the back of his mind.

The Krytheons were only a dream, as was the village in the trees. Dreams of hope and failure. Bove decided he was too tired. He was due for some time off and he needed it. He was dreaming up aliens and living forests. *Maybe I'm losing it,* he wondered. Yet his dreams would not leave him, they continued to draw his attention; they demanded an audience.

And when he gave them a voice, they seemed real, alive. Kabluff sat across from him; it was a memory, not a dream. Yet they were dreams, he fell asleep on his cot and woke on his cot. Dreams of reality.

Steps came back into the tent. "How are you coming with the data?" He sat across from Bove.

"It's fine," Bove said.

"I need your help out there. Everything's ready to load into the shuttle. So, if you're done looking at that stuff could you help out?"

"Yeah." Bove sat back irritated at Steps breaking into his thoughts. "Yeah, I'll be out there in a minute."

"I need you now," Steps stood to leave.

"I said I would be there in a minute." Bove glared at him.

"Fine. Take your time. We can load up tomorrow if that works for you." Steps left.

Bove dropped his head onto his arms on

the table.

Or maybe he was supposed to act on his own and trust the others would do the same. Believe, have faith in his dreams and everything would be fine, or would it? If his dreams were true, the Krytheons would become Gods and that was scary. His dreams showed madness and annihilation. *Is that what I want in a God?*

And if mankind came to Kryth or Gamma-4, would we really annihilate the intelligent life?

Bove raised his head and took a deep breath. Steps was right, the shuttle needed to be loaded so they could leave tomorrow. He went out and spotted Steps sitting on the loading ramp.

This is madness, dreams are dreams, nothing more. He thought. Their work was done. Their ruin had yielded nothing, not a single artifact, and the sensors had been recording for several days. There would be more than enough data to decide about the site. And it would show a planet ideal for colonization. That was the only way to describe it.

Bove sat next to Steps and nodded to the crates waiting to be loaded.

"Yeah," Steps said.

They looked into the forest toward the ruins. The trees stood dark green and brown protecting what lived within them. Bove wondered what lived deep among the trees—an advanced civilization or birds and monkeys? Whatever did, the planet was a paradise. *Yes*, Bove thought. *Ideal.*

Eight

After loading the shuttle, they spent their final night in an empty tent. Bove was restless and unable to get soundly to sleep. Morning came too early for him, but Steps seemed ready to get moving. They broke down the tent and packed it and its contents into the shuttle. Once that was completed it was time to go.

They boarded and strapped themselves in. Bove started the maneuvering thrusters and the shuttle lifted vertically a hundred meters above the ground. He fired the main thruster sending the shuttle in an arc heading up and over the trees. The thruster continued to fire, and the pressure continued to increase until the shuttle reached orbital velocity, then the pressure eased and disappeared when they achieved orbit.

They had six hours of catching up to reach the Mars, so they slept and woke with the alarm that beeped to alert them to their approach.

Bove guided the shuttle into the landing bay and set it down on the bay floor. They were the last shuttle to return, and they had arrived only moments after the others. The outer landing bay door slid down and sealed allowing the pressurization of the shuttle bay. As soon as the atmosphere was established, the shuttle doors opened. Bove and Steps disembarked and headed for their quarters.

Bove entered his room and checked his message terminal, his only message said, *Reports are due by fifteen-thirty hours and de-briefing at sixteen hundred hours*, he checked his timer, fourteen-thirty. *Great*, he thought, *an hour and a half.*

He was not looking forward to the de-briefing. This whole mission did not feel right. They had been told not to make contact -- why? And he had not, it was Kabluff that had contacted him, and maybe others. Now they were not supposed to report that, why? There were too many questions and no answers.

They were professionals, dedicated to the Manifest. They had been in worse situations, at least he had. He had encountered primitive life that had not stopped a colony, they just pushed it aside. *It will benefit the native life for us to be there*, he had been told, and it may well have. It gave them a foot up on other worlds, showed them what can be, and gave them an edge to achieve that. But was that truly beneficial? In the past primitives did benefit, but could not sustain development, for they did not have the background to move forward.

Kabluff and the Krytheons were not primitive. They would not be pushed aside if they were real. But he was only in Bove's dreams, yet Bove could not keep him out of his thoughts, and he did not know why. Was Kabluff real, had it been true that Kabluff was here and there at once, as he said Bove was? Was life on this world vastly superior, pure energy able to be everywhere at once? Did time have no meaning to them, were past and present one and the same? Different sides to the same moon?

Would Bove commit them to extinction? He wished he knew.

His timer chimed.

The de-briefing was short and to the point. a job well done. Everyone reported no evidence of advanced life and suitability for colonization. "We'll be back in three weeks," Kramer said. "And you will be free to go back to your previous assignments." He looked over the room quickly, "Dismissed," he said.

That was it. You go down, report what you see, and do not question. Another assignment was completed, and now it was time for some R&R. What was done, is done, and that was reality, not dreams. Yet Bove was not sure....

Part Two
Three Hills

Nine

Bove stirred and pain shot up his arm. He winced. He shifted to ease the pressure against his side causing a stab of agony to pierce his chest. "Oooh," he moaned, rolling onto his back. The miasma mixed with fresh grass burned his nostrils and under his right hand, he felt grass. The slate gray of pre-dawn colored a sky framed by tall sage grass rising two meters above him. *What? Where am I?* He closed his eyes, rubbed his hand over his face, pinched his nose to kill the smell, then looked again. The sage grass gave off a quiet rustle as it shifted from a slight breeze; the stench pressed into his nose leaving an acidity in his throat. He shivered and tried to sit up. The pain shot from his gut to his chest and across his shoulders. He flopped back on the grass holding his breath with his teeth clamped tight to stifle a scream. The pain eased off.

He lifted his left arm thinking it was asleep but saw a cast covering it to the elbow. He looked to his feet noting that another cast weighed down his right foot. *What the hell!? What's going on?* He tried to remember what had happened to place him in the middle of the tall grass before dawn, but all he could recall was his debriefing on the starship Mars after the mission and even that was foggy. He rolled to his right side ignoring the pain in his chest and arm. He pushed into a sitting position. Again, the pain pulsed through his chest and side, he held his breath while it eased. With his right leg straight in front of him and his left foot under his right knee, he pushed with his right hand and left foot into a standing position. His head felt light as he unsteadily reached for support to balance and found nothing. He stumbled a bit trying to keep the pressure off his right foot and remained standing. Slowly, he eased his weight onto his right foot, expecting shooting pains to rush up his leg, but it was tolerable, and what little pain there was, eased off as he stood there.

A small brown pack sat in the grass next to his feet, the companion boot to the one on his left foot sat next to it. He picked up both, opened the pack to find two energy bars and a red bandana, then shoved the boot into it. *Great*, he thought, *two energy bars, no water, and stuck on a foreign planet. Why?*

The sun had broken the horizon, turning the eastern sky from gray to the light blue of morning. Mountains lined the distant horizon to the northeast with morning shadows shrouding them giving them a sinister look. Below the mountains, grassland dotted with Chaparral bushes and low hills stood in relief in the morning sunlight. The grasslands wrapped around to the south and as Bove turned to his right three large hills came into view.

The closest partially hid the other two, yet Bove could see the jagged sides leading to rocky crests. The first hill had a path curving to the right and at the apex was a small shrine-like building. Looking closer at the other two hills he could make out similar structures sitting on their summits.

Hmm, he thought, *looks like that's the way to*

go.

He pushed aside the grass took a step on his right foot to test the cast while clamping his teeth tight in anticipation of pain. It didn't come. He eased his weight down and took a step only to find he was standing at the edge of a bog. The dark, still water gave off an odor of rot and death. Within its blackness he saw human remains in various stages of decay, empty eye sockets stared up at him as if to invite him to join them. He stumbled back from the sight holding his breath while covering his nose and mouth in disgust. *Where the hell am I,* he thought. Slowly the air slipped out of his lungs causing no pain, but when he drew more, pain cut into him so he could barely stand. He waited until it subsided then took small breaths wincing at the taste and smell. *How do I get out of this cesspool?* He wondered.

The tall sage grass hiding the edge of the water had to be separated to see where the ground ended and the stagnate water began. The smell surrounded him burning into his nostrils and throat. He swallowed to get the taste cleared from his palate, then hobbled to the east along the bank. The water guided him away from the hills, yet he hoped it would lead him out of the bog. If not, he would have to cut through the water hoping for the best.

As he slowly moved along the water's edge the memory of yesterday's events began to crystalize. It had been a standard debriefing with the teams, including himself, stating the planet was good for colonization. He had not mentioned the visions he had while on Kryth. *Yeah, Kryth, not the Delta planet as the company referred to it, But why Kryth? Where had that come from?*

It was after the debriefing that things turned bad. He had returned to his quarters and tried to get some rest, but the visions kept playing in his head, pushing him to tell someone and keeping him awake.

While thoughts of the previous day floated in his mind, he lost sight of where he was. He stopped ready to put his injured foot into the bog water, *Gotta pay closer attention*, he thought, pulling back from the dark pool. He pushed the tall grass aside and proceeded along the bank letting his thoughts continue.

He had gone to the commissary intending to get drunk to forget the visions. Apparently his plan had worked since he could not remember anything after ordering his first drink. The visions and his failure to mention them ate at him until the drink consumed him and the memories were lost in a fog of despair.

A dull pain was throbbing in his ankle, so he stopped to assess his position relative to the hills. They were further behind him. He scanned for any landmark indicating how far he had to go and that was when he saw the eagle.

It was off to the west and its contrast with the blue sky made it stand out against the morning sunlight. Its huge wings stretched at least ten meters and held an updraft as it glided towards him. Its head turned left then right searching the ground below while its wingtips flared turning it directly at him. Its eyes fixed on Bove and held steady as it slowly approached.

A shiver ran across Bove's shoulders as he lowered to the ground letting the grass close over him. The pains in his chest and shoulders had eased to a dull throb, but his foot and arm still hurt. It felt good to be off his foot.

What was that? he wondered. *The thing was*

huge! He peered through the tall grass scanning the sky for the eagle but was unable to spot it. He lay back on the grass, the scent of death mixed with new grass pressing on him like a heavy fog; memories returned. He had been with a dark-haired woman whose honey-brown eyes invited him to her. They got very friendly then someone else took exception to his advances. That started the fight. Anger flared in his thoughts at the memory then faded as he pushed them away remembering where he was.

He pushed himself up again searching the sky for the eagle as he struggled to get to his feet again. His arm and foot hurt and when he put weight on his cast the pain shot up his leg. He stood on shaky legs grinding his teeth until the pain subsided. Slowly his mind accepted the pain enabling him to take a step. He checked the sky again and then located the hills which seemed farther than before. As he proceeded memories filtered back into his mind.

The altercation began with a pushing match that caused Bove to stumble against a pool table. He had taken a swing at his opponent completely missing and was answered with a pool cue arching at his head. His forearm suffered two fractures when he used it to deflect the cue. He fell back and his attacker stepped on his ankle cracking three bones. A punch to his right eye was followed by another into his ribs. That was the last thing he remembered before waking in the putrid bog! He stopped. *Another chance with that guy is what I need*, he thought taking a deep breath and holding it to soothe his chest. He coughed up the vile taste of death permeating the air, then gasped wrapping his arms around his chest. His eyes watered while the pains eased. He stumbled, clenching his teeth, and closing his eyes. Air eased from his lungs, and he rubbed his eyes to clear the tears, then spat the vile taste from his mouth.

Raising his head to see where he was, he noted the hills were ahead of him, four or five kilometers away. He checked the sky only to find the eagle gone. *Good*, he thought. *Maybe it's gone for good.* He tested his foot, then continued even though each step sent sharp pains shooting up his leg and his arm ached under his cast. He wondered who put him in this place, probably the idiot that he got in a fight with, *the nerve of him, or was it someone on the team?* But did it matter?

A shadow slid over him. Looking up, he saw the eagle gliding to the south. It was well over ten meters from wingtip to wingtip. Its head and tail were covered in white feathers, its wings and body had deep brown feathers and its light orange beak extended half a meter ending in a sharp curved point that looked as if it could rip its prey to pieces. Against its underside lay its feet, the same light orange as its beak and tipped with sharp black talons. Its tail feathers shifted slightly keeping it on a steady course as it swiveled its head back and forth searching for prey—rabbits, deer, Bove...

Bove dropped to the ground using his good arm to break his fall and rolled to ease the impact. The drop knocked his breath out and sent daggers of pain through his chest. He gasped not moving.

The eagle slowly turned heading back toward Bove searching until its dark eyes focused on him. It circled once—twice—keeping Bove pinned to the ground with hungry unwavering eyes. Then it turned and glided to the north pumping its wings twice in slow easy strokes.

Bove let the air out of his lungs and slowly inhaled more letting the pain in his chest ease away. Staggering to his feet he pushed on, finding he had wandered a twisting path to where he could see over the tall grass to what looked like a small building. Rounding a curve in the path he saw the stone structure marking the end of the bog. It was a small structure standing about three meters from the apex to the ground. It was supported by columns on each corner engraved with a variety of animals climbing them. There were lions, bears, eagles, frogs, and small creatures on the ground. The roof was a round dome sloping up to a peak at the top. Through the arched doorway and out the opposite side was a path leading to the first hill. In the center of the room was a fountain bubbling water up six or seven centimeters and splashing back into a clear pool. His mouth watered at the thought of clean cool water running down his throat, washing out the stench and taste of the bog.

Ten

After taking a long drink from the fountain Bove looked around. A stone bench circled the interior walls enclosing the fountain. The floor was made of smooth stone, cool through the sole of his boot, he collapsed onto the bench letting the cool of the stone seep into his back. He pressed his arm against himself holding the cast close to his chest while stretching out his leg to ease the pressure. He closed his eyes, took a deep breath letting the clear air fill his lungs. He took another breath savoring the absence of the stench and lack of the taste of death on his tongue. He let the pain in his arm and leg ease. While it slipped away, he felt he could sleep a long, and restful sleep. *But now is not the time to sleep*, he thought, *now I must tend to my situation*. He gazed at the walls in front of him covered with murals of a lush forest of tall trees, deep brown trunks raising into a dense green canopy, like the forest on Gamma-Delta. In the sky above the forest flew birds of many colors and types Bove knew nothing of, except for the eagle which dominated the sky high above the treetops. As he scanned the room, the mural changed from a thick forest to a rocky plain like what Bove could see out the opposite archway toward the hill. In the mural, lion-like creatures roamed among the rocks while scorpions, ants, beetles, lizards, and other small animals covered the ground. *Here and there*, he thought abstractly.

He closed his eyes, leaning back and laying his injured leg on the bench and his arm on his lap. His pain continued to seep away as he tried to figure out who would have dumped him here, and why. The only interaction he had had was with the jerk defending his woman—as if she were incapable of taking care of herself.

"You worry," a voice cut into his thoughts.

Bove jerked to his feet, gasped, held his chest and breath while pain shot up his leg. Across the room stood a slim man dressed in a robe of varied colored strips that blended into a collage rippling from green to blue and into orange then red. It dazzled Bove, causing him to blink his eyes clearing his mind. The man was tall with gray hair, a short beard below a firm straight mouth, a sharp nose, and eyes that bore into Bove like knives of blue ice as he studied Bove like a lab specimen.

"Who…" Bove started but was cut off.

"I am Tanka," the man said stepping toward Bove. "And you wonder why you are here." His blue eyes searched Bove's face, "Yes," he said sitting on the stone bench. "Please sit. Your leg must cause you great pain."

Bove dropped back to the stone bench releasing the pressure on his foot. "Oooh," he gasped.

"Drink, the water will refresh and give you strength," Tanka gestured to a cup of water next to Bove.

Bove glanced down to see a brass cup filled with water on the bench next to him. He hesitated, wondering how it got there, then pushed aside the mystery and picked up the cup. The water was sweet and cool, and vitalize his arms and legs, easing the pain.

"We brought you here for redemption," Tanka studied Bove.

"You brought me here?" Stunned, Bove looked up at Tanka, "Who are you?"

"I am Tanka." He eyed Bove as if he were stupid.

"Yeah, so you said, but..."

"You are here for redemption." Tanka cut him off and stood up.

Bove stared at him at a loss, *who is this guy? Why is he saying I'm here for redemption? Is he from the ship?* "I mean," Bove stated, "what's your purpose, what do you do? Are you from the ship? Because you don't look like it?"

"I am your guide on the path to redemption." Tanka gazed down at Bove.

"Redemption?" Bove asked, "For what?"

"If you choose to follow the path much will be explained."

"And if I don't?" Bove looked up to meet Tanka's eyes.

"If you choose to not follow the path you must return to the bog, and the bog is where you will remain." Tanka strolled around the fountain to the opposite exit.

Bove looked at him. "How do I get off this place?" he asked, "I need to get back to the ship if it hasn't gone on without me. I doubt they are sitting in orbit waiting for me to follow your path. So, tell me, how do I get off this world and back on my way home?"

"You have only two choices," Tanka raised his

hand toward the exit behind him, "the path to redemption or," he pointed out the exit behind Bove, "the bog."

"That's ludicrous!" Bove sat up straight and glared at Tanka. "I demand to be returned to my ship! I won't follow your path or return to the putrid bog, and I don't need to be redeemed. Tell me how to get to my ship!"

Tanka studied Bove across the small room, "It's understandable you are upset," he said, "but everything will be explained if you choose to follow the path. If you refuse your only choice will be to return to the bog."

Tanka lifted his arm waving it toward the exit to the first hill. When Bove looked the opening was covered with a painted wall of trees and animals.

"You see," Tanka said, "your only exit is to the bog. Let me tell you of the bog. The water is deadly to drink and if you get into it, it will seep into your skin poisoning you slowly. You may survive the bog a few days, but no longer. That is why it would be wise to choose the path to redemption." He studied Bove for a moment then added, "You didn't get in the water, did you?" Bove shook his head.

"Ah, that's good." Tanka nodded and watched Bove absorbing the information and when he knew Bove understood he sat, "Come sit next to me while I explain what you must do."

Bove looked at Tanka holding his anger in check while trying to suppress the pain shooting up his leg. He could not help wondering what was going on. He was brought here by Tanka, why? And why was Tanka conveniently offering redemption, for what? Yet Tanka seemed familiar like Bove had met him before, but where?

"Come," Tanka said, "and all will be explained."

Bove stared at him, *explained?* he wondered. "What's to be explained? I'm here by mistake," he said, "You must have gotten the wrong guy. You should send me back and get the right guy."

"I have the right *guy*," Tanka said. "And you must choose the path of redemption. Come, sit and commit to your choice."

"Commit?"

"Yes, come sit." Tanka motioned to Bove to come to him.

Bove leaned back on the bench watching Tanka.

"No, sit here," Tanka said, indicating the bench opposite Bove, the seat on the other side of the room.

Bove sat for a moment confused; forcing himself to his feet he took the five steps across the room to sit next to Tanka, "Okay?"

"Good," Tanka said. "You have committed."

Bove looked at him then back toward the opening to the bog, where only a wall painted with tall grass and birds appeared. He turned to the opposite doorway to see the path to the three hills. "What…" he started.

"You've chosen the path to redemption, so the past is closed. The path will heal and protect you for as long as you stay true to it. At the end, you will know what you must do to redeem yourself."

"What I want is to get back to my ship, so how do I do that?"

"To return to your ship you must follow the path and accept redemption."

"What do I need redemption for?" Bove asked,

"I've done nothing."

"That's what the path will tell you. You are in a WayGate which allows passage to resume the path. If you leave a WayGate through the same doorway you entered, you will not be allowed to continue. On the hills, you will encounter CrossGates that allow you to cross the path in a single direction. And at each hill's summit, you will find a TempleGate where you will receive instruction for your redemption." Tanka stood and stepped to the fountain then turned to Bove. "Each of these gates, like this WayGate, will allow one-way passage. Follow the path over the hills," he said pointing to the exit, "and you will find yourself home."

Bove looked out the exit, "Home?" he asked and turned to face Tanka, but he was gone. Bove looked around; the only exit was toward the first hill. On the opposite wall was a mural covering the doorway to the bog. The stone fountain gurgled splashing clear freshwater into its basin.

Realizing how thirsty he was, he stepped to the fountain and drank his fill, in case it would be the last until he was over the hills. Gazing out the doorway he felt better, his leg was throbbing like it had when he arrived, but his chest and arm felt normal.

Okay, he thought, *follow the path to get home. How that will work is a mystery, but it appears to be the only option.* Glancing back where the entrance to the Bog had been, he felt satisfied, then stepped out of the doorway to the first hill.

Eleven

A tingle, like a warm chill, ran through his body, spinning his head with a slight dizziness. He felt a little disorganized--unsettled, then it passed returning to normal. The sun was twenty-five degrees above the horizon and the air was dry. The dirt path, a simple trail beaten smooth by hundreds of feet, led to the first hill. Bove looked around at the flat plain stretching out to the left and right. It was covered with boulders varying from three to four meters high, to small stones scattered about—like an asteroid field. There were no trees or bushes, and no sign of animals, only the barren land of rocks. He gazed at the rocks wondering why he felt better after his brief rest in the WayGate. His foot had turned into a dull ache and the needles piercing his arm were gone. He felt good! *Funny*, he thought, *why would I think of it as a WayGate?*

In the distance was another WayGate like the one he just stepped from, and beyond, the path continued to the first hill where another WayGate sat at its base.

Bove sighed stepping forward on the path. A light breeze stirred up dust around the rocks and cooled him. It gave him a boost to proceed at a steady pace, though slow due to his injured foot.

He panned across the rocky plain and caught a

movement close to a large rock on his left, glancing back nothing was there. He watched and shortly a lion-like creature stepped from behind a boulder. It was at least four meters from head to tail. Its shoulders were rippling with muscles. Its thick powerful front legs ended in broad paws. Its back was covered with dark fur spreading over its haunches and onto its powerful back legs. Its tail, adding another two meters to its length, switched slowly as the creature turned its head towards Bove. Its snout was short like a lion's and its forehead was topped with large ears that angled up sharply like a wolf's. They twisted back and forth searching for any sound. Its eyes fixed on Bove holding him in place while its tongue licked out over its lips. It roared showing sharp incisors on both the top and bottom of its jaws. One giant paw stroked the air baring sharp claws—as if waving to Bove. A shiver ran up Bove's back leaving a prickling feeling at the nape of his neck.

The beast turned back to the rock and clawed at its base, seeming to forget Bove. He relaxed, let out his breath, and felt a sharp pain shoot through his chest. Both his arm and leg were hurting, and he was feeling tired. He wanted to rest even though he was quite far from the next WayGate.

He glanced back but the creature was nowhere in sight. "Good," he mumbled, "I hope it stays gone." As he pushed on towards the WayGate keeping a watchful eye for the beast in case it approached. Yet he let his thoughts drift to distract him from his current situation. How he got here eluded him. He was sure he would find out once over these three hills. Yet he wondered why he felt he had to get over them. Why could he not wait to be picked up; was there someone over the last hill to take him back to the ship? He knew he had to follow the path but was not sure why.

The WayGate halfway to the first hill was like the one by the bog—murals on the walls and a fountain in the center. The murals were different, the dome was painted with storm clouds with no birds, the walls were covered with snow-capped mountains seen from such a great distance nothing was discernible in any detail. In the foreground were rocks like the ones covering the plain outside. There were doorways, where he entered and one leading to the first hill.

He collapsed on the stone bench that wrapped around the inside of the WayGate. His leg and arm were hurting, but his chest felt better—no pains when he moved. He was able to lift his arm without his chest hurting. He eyed the fountain knowing the water would not come to him yet wanting to rest where he sat.

After a few minutes he was feeling better; his pains had eased, and his mind had cleared. He was feeling like he could make more than a kilometer without fainting. His leg didn't hurt when he stepped to the fountain where the cool freshwater bubbled into a pool. Taking a small sip of the water eased his dry throat and he felt his strength return.

Refreshed he stepped out onto the path once again, glancing back he knew the doorway into the WayGate would be gone, in its place was only a wall covered with carvings of small animals digging around small trees.

Trees? Bove thought. He had not seen trees anywhere on his way to the WayGate. He looked around. Scattered across the plain between the rocks were small Joshua-like trees dotting the landscape. None were more than three to four meters high. Their branches spread out no farther than their height providing areas of shade. Little pools of coolness.

That's a change, he thought as he stepped forward. The first hill was much closer and seemed to have grown higher. He looked around as he made his way along the path watching for the eagle and the lion creature. He saw no sign of either. That gave him a little relief knowing they were not waiting close-by to jump him.

Keeping watch along the path for about ten meters on each side he saw a fallen branch from one of the small trees. It was a short distance from the path and looked about the right size to make a good walking stick. It would help ease the stress on his leg. Stepping off the path towards the tree he noticed movement in the branches. *Something is in there*, he thought stopping to study the tree. *It can't be large*, he calmed himself noting the small size of the tree and continued slowly across the gap toward the stick.

As he approached, he noticed bugs moving around on the ground, one scurried across the top of his cast. It looked like a scorpion, a shorter tail, and no pinchers. He kicked his foot to be sure the thing was gone. Ants were running over the boot on his left foot. He stamped it doing little good, they still swarmed over and up his boot.

Well, he thought, *maybe they don't sting*.

They did!

"Ow!" he cried and stamped his foot again. Thankfully, they were not on his injured foot where they could crawl under the cast and sting. He reached with his good right hand and slapped the ants from his leg and having cleared them from his pants he looked up to see a big bobcat like animal with a long tail sitting on one of the lower branches in the tree. It snarled at him as much as to say, *stay away, this is my tree!* Bove stood silent and unmoving looking the cat straight in the eyes, the cat didn't flinch.

The stick Bove had come for was laying a meter and a half from where he stood, and it did look like a good walking stick. He only had to take another step, reach down, and pick it up, then retreat to the path. If he could get a handle on it, he would have a weapon to use if the bobcat were to attack him. With that in mind, he stepped to the stick and bend to pick it up. That was when the bobcat jumped!

Bove was looking at the stick to be sure to get a good grip on it when he heard the bobcat growl as it sprang from the branch. He fell to his left grabbing the stick with his right hand and rolling onto his shoulder— pains shot through his left arm and into his chest. He ignored them. As he rolled, he brought the stick up in an arc passing through the air where he had been standing.

He missed the bobcat's body but caught its tail, knocking it off balance. It let out a screech and twisted to land on its feet about a meter from where Bove lay. It snarled ready to pounce then hesitated as Bove leveled his new staff at him. It looked Bove in the eye—its tail swinging slowly side to side as it considered its options.

Slowly Bove pushed himself to his feet farther from the bobcat, not losing eye contact. The bobcat growled deep in its throat holding its ground, its tail continued to slowly swish, left then right. Bove took another step back pointing the stick directly at it. They stayed status quo; until the next step, the bobcat attacked the stick swapping its claw against it and knocking it to the right. Bove held on but lost his balance and when he put his leg out to stop himself a pain shot up to his hip and he fell to the ground dropping his staff.

The bobcat jumped. Bove raised his left arm for protection as the bobcat landed on top of him. It sank its teeth deep into the cast and snarled. Bove hit it with his fist and shook his arm trying to free it. He rolled over to free his right arm and grasping the staff he struck hard on the bobcat's back and shook his arm again. The bobcat came loose and as Bove struggled to his feet the cat backed away, swapping at the stick pointed at him. Bove pushed the stick at the bobcat and yelled "Aaaah! Aaaah!" Scaring it back up the tree into the high branches.

That was when Bove realized there were ants on him, and they were stinging his arms and legs. He yelped and stomped his feet ignoring the pain in his right foot and shook his arms trying to throw the ants off. He stumbled back toward the path shaking his arms and legs as he went. *Luckly*, he thought, *the scorpion isn't on me*. At least he hoped it wasn't. The ants were falling off as he approached the path, yet the stings were like fire on his arms and legs, and he thought he could feel them running over him. He rubbed himself as best he could to kill the feeling.

When he reached the path and fell onto it, the ants were gone, and the stings were burning less. The feeling that ants were on him persisted and he had to convince himself they were gone. He worked at that as he got to his feet and continued toward the first hill—thankful it was not the eagle or lion creature that was after him.

The branch did turn out to be a good walking stick, it was slightly taller than Bove and the bark was worn off making the wood smooth. It was the right size for a firm hold with one hand. He walked much easier using his staff as support when he stepped on his right foot. He was able to cover more ground quicker and before he realized he was standing before the WayGate leading to the first hill. Even though he had the support of the staff his right leg still ached. Although his arm did not hurt much considering the oversized bobcat had bitten into the cast and jerked it around. *Strange*, he thought as he stepped into the WayGate and sank onto the stone bench.

The walls of this WayGate were a single mural wrapping around the entire room picturing the three hills. Winding up each hill was the path and between the hills were various landscapes. The first, at the bottom of the first hill, was covered with boulders and small bushes. Between the second and third hills was a plain of large trees and bushes, and after the third hill were small trees ending at a bluff overlooking a river. The path ran down the bluff to the riverbank and disappeared in a grove of tall trees. In the distance was a waterfall.

Bove wondered how close to reality the mural was. After a brief rest, he rose and stepped to the fountain for a drink. As before the water was cool and refreshing making him feel renewed and able to continue for hours. He stepped out the doorway and glancing back saw the entry door had become part of the mural leaving his only option to continue up the hill.

Twelve

The path curved to the right ascending the hill and halfway up was a CrossGate, *more rest and refreshment*, Bove thought as he stepped out into the sunlight. The incline was not too bad and with his walking stick, he was able to move along easily. His leg did not hurt as much as it had, and the pain in his arm was nearly gone.

About halfway to the WayGate, the eagle glided across the plain above the trees, its head slowly swinging from side to side searching. It was enormous and Bove eased down making himself as small as possible, not moving and barely breathing. The eagle continued straight toward him. There was nowhere to hide, only the path—no trees or big rocks! *Don't move*, he thought, eyes locked on the eagle.

It continued slowly hardly seeming to move. When it was within twenty meters it tilted its wings back and dropped to the ground landing on its feet, while its wings closed against its sides. It hardly made a sound and stared directly at Bove sending shivers over his shoulders causing the muscles in his back and arms to tighten—he gripped his staff until his knuckles turned white.

The eagle did not approach; it merely looked at Bove knowingly, as if to appraise him, perhaps for a meal? Bove had nowhere to go, no place to hide; he was totally in the open and defenseless. He gripped his staff harder and wanted to look away from the eagle's eyes that held him. He felt like it knew his thoughts, his feelings, and his terror. Suddenly it spread its wings, pushed into the air toward Bove. It tucked its feet against its belly and made one strong stroke downward with its wings coming directly at Bove. A second push of its wings raised it above Bove's head, and it glided past turning back toward the plain.

Bove's heart was pounding, his head was spinning, and he let out a gasp, drew in a breath realizing he had not breathed the whole time the eagle sat staring at him. *My God! That can't happen again!* he thought, trying to get control of himself, *it could have killed me in a heartbeat!* He looked up and saw the eagle was gliding to the east low to the ground.

Up the hill the CrossGate was close. Bove continued up at a much faster pace. His heart slowed and the muscles in his back and arms eased. His thoughts shifted from the eagle, which was now out of sight, to the CrossGate ahead. This gate resembled the others with carvings on the outside and murals on the inside. He hardly noticed them as he sank to the bench to rest after having a cool drink from the center fountain.

There was no more sign of the eagle the rest of the way to the summit where a much larger TempleGate stood. Four round columns at least four meters from the base to the top supported a round roof pitching up to a peak. The columns lined the front surrounding the doorway and were covered with animal carvings, as were the walls behind the columns. As Bove studied them he noticed the eagle high up the column on the left and the lion creature at the base of the right column. The oversized bobcat lurked in a tree as he had found it, and at the base of each column were beetles, ants, scorpions, and any number of other bugs that had annoyed him when he obtained his staff. In addition to those, there were multitudes of other animals from birds of varied sizes and colors carved at the tops of the columns to tigers, bear-like creatures, and other large animals like elephants or rhinoceroses circling the lower parts of the columns.

Bove shivered at the thought of the things waiting to get to him, and the memory of the ants crawling over him, he felt some now, even though the burning from the bites was gone. Rubbing his arms and shoulders eased the feeling until it was cleared. He made one last check for the eagle and stepped out of the sun and into the TempleGate.

The morning heat dissipated—like there was a cooling system, but Bove had seen no indication of technology since his arrival. *Must be the shade,* he thought. The stone floor felt cool even through his boot and cast and the fountain in the center of the room looked refreshing. The walls were circled with a stone bench and the rest of the temple was bare except for the murals covering the walls. The picture was the forest of giant trees displayed in the other gates. In a clearing nestled among the trees was a village filled with people engaged in their daily activities of mending wagons, carrying goods to their homes, children playing in the empty areas between buildings. People visiting outside stores. A thriving village like the empty village Bove had investigated on Kryth, where this began. On the dome was a clear sky with a couple of puffy clouds.

What is the meaning of this? he wondered, *this*

place, the murals, the fact I am here? He eased himself onto the stone bench feeling more tired than he realized; both his arm and leg were hurting. He had been so focused on getting up the hill away from the eagle that he had forgotten about his injuries; now the pain was back. He closed his eyes and let his mind drift.

"Rest and be healed."

Bove jerked his head around to the sound and was startled to see Tanka standing on the other side of the TempleGate. He wore a green robe that shimmered in the light, it changed from dark emerald green to the light green of new leaves. It dazzled Bove causing him to drop his eyes to Tanka's feet which were covered with brown sandals. Gazing up again, Bove came to Tanka's face; muscles taut with a grim line for his mouth and creases joining his eyebrows. His gaze was fixed on Bove causing a ripple of unsettling to course through him. Bove remembered their conversation in the WayGate outside the bog. He straightened into a sitting position and Tanka's face relaxed, a slight smile curved his lips when he said, "I see you are better, that's good. You have stayed the path well. I welcome you to the TempleGate of Acceptance. It is here you will come to understand and accept your deeds requiring redemption."

Bove could not understand how Tanka had arrived here; he had not passed Bove on the path. *Is this a vision?* He wondered.

"You look confused," Tanka said, "but be assured you will understand in time."

"Understand what?" Bove asked. "Redemption? For what? What is it you think I have done?"

"*Not* done," Tanka said, "Not done."

"Not done?"

"Yes, but first come and drink of the water to refresh you. Ease your mind to be more open to the reality of your deeds. Please. Drink," Tanka said offering a cup of water to Bove.

Bove looked at the cup, wondering what he needed redemption for, and took it knowing he may be making a big mistake, but he was thirsty and tired and hurting and wanted nothing more than a little rest.

"Good," Tanka said.

The water felt good in his throat and cool as it wet his dryness. He felt as if he could fall to sleep for days. The pains in his arm, leg, and chest eased slipping away and his worries seemed minor, almost nonexistent. He laid his head back and closed his eyes to his troubles.

"Watch," Tanka said as he sat beside Bove, you will see the errors of what you have done. Tanka waved his arm in front of them and nodded toward the far wall.

The wall was covered with a forest of trees, tall like the trees on Gamma-Delta. They rose hundreds of times the height of the people standing at their base. The trees reached more than three hundred meters into the sky. The people looked like ants below them.

They were beautiful! They were the trees of Kryth, the forest surrounding the camp he and Steps had made on Gamma-Delta. The same forest where his visions occurred.

Bove watched as the people walked to a small village of scattered huts with gardens and barns in a clearing in the forest. They went about their business, fetching water, tending their gardens, caring for their livestock.

The picture changed. The people remained, but they were no longer tending fields and life stock. They were ascending to the trees. Long ropes extended from the tops of the trees to the forest floor where the people attached their belongings and watched as they were raised to the treetops. The people were being raised in baskets, up to join their possessions.

The picture changed again. In the treetops, the foliage was thick, and within the dense tree limbs and leaves, the people were making huts with leaves forming the roofs and walls. Large planks were laid across branches to form floors and walkways between the trees. Slowly a village emerged under the canopy, bigger buildings for meeting places and smaller ones for living huts. Staircases twisting around the tree trunks leading to other rooms and structures higher up. The people had moved to the trees and were no longer dependent on the ground for safety. They were free from the beasts of the land.

Again, a new picture appeared. And before him was the village in the trees and above were ships skimming across the treetops, beams of light searching below. The people scurried in vain to hide beneath large branches from the searching beams. The ships fired lasers into the trees slicing the branches from the trunks and crashing them to the ground—taking the people hiding with them. The ships came one after another until there were no trees in which to hide. And no people to hide within them.

Bove felt sick. Many of the people were killed, their whole existence destroyed. What would cause such destruction? He turned away from the sight, closing his eyes and remembering the visions from Kryth. The same scenes as displayed on the wall, the same story he had received on Kryth. The warning he chose to ignore when he recommended colonization.

"Closing your eyes will not change what is to be," Tanka said. "What you have seen is the reality of your choices. Choices you must be redeemed for if you want to survive."

"What…" Bove was disorientated by the pictures. "What do you mean to *survive*?"

"Bove," Tanka continued, "you have made a decision that affects everyone residing on what you call the Delta Planet. You have ignored the warnings we gave while you were there. Do you not remember?" Tanka looked at Bove questions dancing in his eyes waiting for Bove to understand. "We showed you the consequences of your decisions while you were there. Do you not remember?"

Shock and understanding ran through Bove! *What have I done?* He thought. *What has happened because of me?* He dropped his head into his hands forcing the thoughts out of his head, the images of the people crashing to the ground, burning in the fires from the ships, and dying because of him. "Oh, what have I done?" he moaned, "What have I done?"

"Yes," Tanka said. "You made a decision with severe consequences you cannot change, but you can be redeemed for your decision. And the first step to redemption is acceptance."

"But what you showed me, will that come true?"

"Oh, yes. There is nothing to be done to change that. What can be done is to redeem yourself for your foolishness, and your lack of listening and believing in your visions." Tanka watched Bove's indecision reflecting on his face. "First you must accept what you have done. Can you do that?"

Bove looked up, "Accept? Have I not done that

already? Don't I have to live with my decision?"

"Oh, yes you know what you did, but you must accept you have a penance to pay. That is the purpose of your journey on the road to redemption. Your first step is acceptance and that is what you must do."

"Accept what I have done, yes. I can accept that. I must accept that now that you have shown the results of my decision." Bove thought for a moment while Tanka watched, then continued, "But what else could I have done? I would not have been believed if I told of visions—dreams—I had there. I would have been sent to counseling and restricted from additional assignments if I told anyone. I felt my only choice was to give my approval as was expected."

"Ah yes, what was expected. And that is your folly to believe you can only do as is expected, not as you believe is right. And for that, you have a penance to pay."

"And if I don't pay the penance what then? You have no control over me. If this is a vision as before, then what control do you have?"

"I control your destiny and your future. You may not understand, but I assure you things will not go as you wish should you decide against acceptance. Choose wisely, your future depends on it."

Bove glanced towards the floor for a second and when he looked up again Tanka was no longer there, where he had gone Bove had no clue. *Acceptance*, Bove thought, *what does he mean by acceptance? I know what I did, and I accept it, but was it me that has determined the future for them? Or would my input have been ignored had I objected to colonization?* Bove sat contemplating and not coming to any conclusion. *This*, he thought, *is another vision and not even real—a dream. How could I be dropped on some lost planet and not be missed? The Mars would not leave me here. And no one would be able to shuttle me down without the ship knowing what was happening. No, this is not real—I have to wake up.*

He stood stomped his feet and felt a sharp pain shoot up his right leg, He realized if it was a vision, it was very real. He felt back to the bench, bumping his left arm, and feeling pains run up into his shoulder. *Okay*, he thought. *If it's not real, it's a hell of a vision! A vision like the ones on Kryth.*

He sat a few minutes longer not thinking about anything. He gave up on figuring out what was happening. He only knew he must continue to follow the path to the next hill, *where else can I go?* he thought and stood up, assessed his foot by lightly adding pressure on it to be sure it was no worst, then stepping to the water in the center of the room.

He drank enough to satisfy himself, picked up his staff and pack, and stepped to the archway leading out of the TempleGate of Acceptance. *Acceptance*, he thought, what must I accept other than I failed to tell of my visions?

Thirteen

Bove looked through the archway toward the southeast. The sun hung fifty degrees above the horizon filling a cloudless sky with brilliant light and bathing the grassy plain in brilliance. The bog was a stagnate pond sitting in the middle of the vast plain of tall Indian grass and small chaparral bushes standing like forgotten flowers in an abandoned garden. The smell of rot and death from the bog did not reach him, and he smiled at the good fortune. In the distance, a line of mountains ringed the plain and beyond there was only sky. No apparent movement even though he knew the dangers out there from the eagle, the lion creature, the scorpions, and whatever else that could injure or kill him.

The path sloped down to the left in a sharp curve. Below, was the CrossGate he had passed through on his way up. *Weird*, he thought, *I didn't see an opening on this side when I was there, but maybe I missed it.* Past the CrossGate was only the rocky hillside covered with small clumps of sagebrush and stunted Joshua trees. And no movement to the bottom.

He stepped out onto the path. A shiver ran through him not chilling him but causing a slight disorientation, a disruption in his thoughts causing him not to remember anything about the TempleGate of

Acceptance other than having been inside. The shiver passed, and he shook his head in bewilderment thinking how funny that feeling was. He headed down the hill toward the CrossGate.

The slope was steeper than he expected and the pressure on his right leg was painful. After a short way, he was limping as the pain ran up his leg and into his hip making it hard to keep a steady pace, but he kept on toward the CrossGate leaning heavily on his staff to keep the pressure off his foot. Fo*llow the path and it will lead you home*. He wondered who had told him that, and as far as he remembered he had not seen another person since he had awakened in the bog. It did seem to make sense that following the path was his only choice. It must lead somewhere, and what was his other option?

It was not long before he reached the CrossGate and sat under the cool cover, refreshed from the clear water in the center of the small room. The only exit was toward the bottom of the hill. *One way in and one way out. Not real, yet not a dream.*

Like his visions on Kryth, although he was not here of his choosing. If whoever put him here would get him back to the ship, he would forget about it. He was not looking for revenge, only to be back on his way home. If he would be picked up and settled on the ship, he would be fine, no hard feelings, no repercussions. If only he could be back on his way. He banged the end of his staff on the floor punctuating his desire to get back on the ship, *come on,* he thought, *show me where the shuttle is, where I have to be for the pickup.*

He leaned back closing his eyes and letting the tension dissipate and after cooling off he stood and drank more water. The pain in his leg was nearly gone, and when he put pressure on his foot, he was surprised the pain did not return, he stepped and felt nothing. He felt like he had when he had started down the hill. *It won't last,* he thought, *but I must continue.*

He picked up his staff, threw his pack over his shoulder, and stepped to the archway. The air was clear, and the sun shined brightly on the rocks making them stand out against the soft brown of the prairie grass. The small Joshua trees cast small shadows like dots on the plain. He turned away gazing toward the next WayGate then stepped onto the path.

As he made his way toward the next gate the pain did not return to his leg, he used his staff to support his weight and tried to keep as little pressure on it as he could. As he descended, he studied the second hill and unlike the first, it was covered with short sawgrass and small sage bushes. Very few rocks of any size were visible. It looked refreshing after the barren hill he was on. Below at the base of the hill was the next WayGate, and from it, the path continued to the left in a winding direction through thick sage and small desert willows. Large rocks clustered near the path hiding it from his view.

As he continued his leg felt stronger with little pain, unlike the first part of his descent. The cast on his left arm was still in one piece even after being chewed up from the bobcat, and he had no pain in the arm. He guessed it was because he had not been using it much. He did feel tired as he approached the WayGate at the base of the hill, and when he stepped into it, he was grateful for the bench as he sank onto it with a sigh.

This gate matched the others with intricate bas-reliefs on the outer walls and murals lining the inner walls. A stone bench circled a small fountain that sat in the center bubbling freshwater, and as he drank, he felt his energy return filling his arms and legs with strength. He sat on the stone bench sliding his pack off his shoulder and laying his staff on the floor at his feet. The air drifting in through the archway of the gate was fresh, clear, and cool.

He breathed deep sucking in the fresh smells of sawgrass and sage crowding the path and covering the hill ahead. The sawgrass was about knee high—enough to hide small animals like snakes or bobcats, and the sages were a meter or two high and sparse. The path disappeared among the bushes a little more than three meters from the gateway—twisting out of sight.

What will happen if I can't get back, he wondered. Various scenarios played in his head, he would have to find shelter and food, and water. He had no weapon to hunt with. Old school would be his option. He had seen no game, but there had to be deer or other large game he could hunt. There was plenty of stones and branches to make weapons, it takes a little ingenuity and practice. Yes, he would be able to survive, yet to what end?

He sat a while longer gathering his strength for the next leg of his journey. This one was over flat ground that should not be a strain on his leg, and the distance to the next hill was approximately a kilometer. *If I keep feeling better,* he thought, *the next hill should be much easier to get up and the one after even easier.* And with that thought, he stood and stepped to the archway leading out

He followed the path and found even though it went into the bushes it was clear and plainly visible as he walked along. Yet he felt a twinge of fear that he would run into another bobcat, or other small animal hiding close by where a quick attack would be hard to defend. He didn't feel like dealing with anything again, not after facing the bobcat on the tree. The lion creature and eagle were entirely different, and he feared for his life if he came across either of them. He tried not to worry about that. What could he do if they wanted to come for him? The smaller animals were of more concern, they could hide in the grass or up the trees and pounce when he was not expecting them. That was where his attention focused.

He continued along with no incidence until he came to several large rocks blocking the path. How they had come to be there he could not imagine since there were no hills close by and no other rocks of any size. What he discovered, after closer inspection, was lightning or another violent event, had caused a large rock to be broken causing its fragments to scatter across the path.

Satisfied with his conclusion he proceeded to look for the best way around the blockage. The left had fewer obstacles, so with his staff, he poked at the grass to scare any animals hiding there, and satisfied the way was clear he stepped off the path and into the grass.

A loud screech pierced his ears jarring his whole body—he froze for a moment unsure of what happened. Quickly he regained his wherewithal and looked up to see the eagle circling. The eagle's eyes were fixed on its prey, and it was heading straight for Bove. For an instant, Bove froze in his boots unable to comprehend what was happening. He could not understand where it had come from, yet it was almost upon him. That was when he realized something had to happen if he were to live another minute. He jumped for the rocks trying to get behind the biggest one he could see and as he leaped for safety the eagle's beak slammed shut in the air he had just vacated!

He tumbled across the ground and stopped behind a decent size rock, looking up he saw the eagle swoop past and lift into the air. It tipped its wing to the left and circled in a tight curve coming around to face him, its eyes were focused squarely on him; its wings were straight out to the sides tipping slightly to keep it directed at him. Its legs were pointed forward talons out and gleaming in the sunlight.

Bove felt his heart race, adrenaline surged through his body, his thoughts circled in his mind searching for an escape. The eagle came closer dropping slightly to align its claws with Bove. A shiver ran through him from the back of his neck to his knees jerking him into motion. He slid his hands down his staff and as the eagle came within reach, he slammed the staff into the side of its legs and dropped to the ground in a single smooth motion. The eagle screeched and tipped to the right, and as it did its claws shifted slightly. Bove raised his left arm to defend himself and one talon slammed into it throwing him back against the rock as pain shot up his arm, and the breath flew from his lungs. A twinge of pain shot through his chest.

The eagle disappeared over his head. He knew the thing was turning to get a better run at him and if he did not move, he would be the eagle's meal. Using his right arm, he pushed himself up onto his feet and looked over the rock to locate the eagle. It was not high or far and turning preparing to make another run at him. He did have the rocks between him and the beast providing protection, but if it landed and came at him on the ground, what protection did he have?

He cursed at the thought and looked over the

rock again to gauge its position. It had turned to the right and was straightening out to come across the path to his side. Bove circled the rock keeping it between him and the eagle. The eagle watched Bove as it glided across the path. Bove was halfway around the rock and standing on the path once again on the far side of the rocks that had blocked his way. He was free to continue to the second hill if he could rid himself of the beast in the sky.

He turned and looked down the path hoping for better shelter, but not expecting it. A short distance away the path turned around some rocks and vanished in the stubby trees beyond. He studied the rocks and determined they were too small to afford any protection from the flying beast—as were the trees. He turned back to check the eagle's position and found it turning to the left around the first hill and as he watched it glided out of sight. He slid to the ground, his back against the rock protecting him, and let out a sigh of relief. Taking a deep breath he felt his shaking ease and as he loosened his grip on his staff, he realized how tense and frightened he was.

Another deep breath caused a pain in his chest, yet it eased his pounding heart and calmed his shaky hands. The tension in his shoulders and back eased. He noticed the cast on his left arm was cracked and it felt loose, *not good,* he thought. He opened his pack, removed the lace from his spare boot, then tied a loop in one end through which he ran the other end. Wrapping it around his cast he pulled the lace tight, circled it around the rest of the cast, and secured the end to hold the cast tightly together. While tightening the lace he noticed his arm was not hurting like he would expect. *That's good*, he thought, *but it probably won't last.*

He made another check of the sky and saw no sign of the eagle. Using his staff, he rose to his feet, took another deep breath to steady himself, and stepped on towards the WayGate at the base of the second hill.

The path was clear the rest of the way and he hurried as best he could on his injured foot, which surprisingly was not hurting as much as he thought it should. *The adrenaline from the eagle attack is keeping the pain at bay*, he thought.

Once at the WayGate, he refreshed himself with the water in the center of the gate then sat on the stone bench enjoying one of his energy bars. *To keep going,* he reasoned. This gate, like the others, had paintings of animals and trees and hills on the walls and ceiling. Out the opposite doorway, Bove could see the path turning to the left as the hill slopped up and out of sight. He rested wondering if he could survive another attack from the eagle.

Yeah, he was lucky the eagle did not pursue him further. If it had landed on the ground and come for him, he would have been done for. *I should have been left with some weapon—a blaster at least—to protect myself. Whoever did this must not care if I survive. They'd have gone on without me, not even knowing I'm missing. Oh, if only I could get my hands on whoever did this...* He sighed. *But to get back I must continue; nothing will be resolved sitting here.*

Once he had convinced himself his only choice was to continue up the hill, he resolved to do whatever it took to make it to the top. And with that, he stood, tested his foot, which felt much better, checked his arm which had no pain, and stepped across the WayGate to the opposite doorway. Glancing back, he saw the doorway where he had entered was a landscape of grass and small trees. The way back was closed, as it had been at each gate.

He stepped out into the sunlight. It was close to noon and the day had heated up. The sun warmed his back as he continued up the path which headed to the left at a steeper angle than the first hill and appeared not to pass through any Gate until the top where the second TempleGate stood leaving him in the open to the hill's crest. An easy target if the eagle returned. He scanned the sky before proceeding and when he saw no sign of the beast, he kept walking briskly up the path. His pace slowed as the path was steep and his foot was not a hundred percent and hurt with each step; *best to take it slow.* He kept a steady pace the rest of the way up the hill and soon found himself standing in front of the TempleGate. It matched the temple on the first hill with large columns supporting a round roof. All the same animal carvings adorned the outer walls with the eagle and lion creature prominent among the carvings. There was a new creature Bove had not noticed on the first temple, it was a huge bear-like monster standing on two legs peering out from the bushes. Its massive head featured sharp incises with a long snout and small beady eyes with a very unfriendly look in them.

Bove sighed.

Fourteen

Stepping into the TempleGate he found the interior matching the gate at the top of the first hill, it was large with similar decorations—carvings on the outside, murals on the inside. Only these murals were of massive trees rising hundreds of meters into the sky. Scattered through the treetops were small and larger huts like meeting rooms. Gazing around the room Bove could see part of the story he had been shown in the first temple. It ended with the people ascending to the village in the treetops.

"You have done well, Bove," Tanka said.

Bove spun around to see Tanka standing on the other side of the fountain. He wore a rode rippling in shades of blue and causing it to change tint as he moved, like waves on a pond. Bove dazzled for a moment, glanced away to regain his composure. He looked at the floor before bringing his eyes back to Tanka's.

"You look better," Tanka said, "How are you feeling?"

"How am I feeling?" Bove said his voice rising, "Don't you know what happened out there? That damn giant eagle nearly killed me! How do you think I feel?" He glared at Tanka and took a deep breath. "Well?" he said.

"The path has hazards, but the beasts are of no consequence."

"What!?" Bove glared at him. He had nearly been killed by the eagle and the Cave Lion seemed much more dangerous. "I was nearly killed!"

"But you remain unharmed," Tanka stated. "Come have a drink and rest," he indicated the place next to him. "You must focus on your redemption and the path to it."

"What am I supposed to do about those beasts?" Bove clinched his fist and then spread his fingers, "Are you not going to help me?"

"Oh, but I am helping. You have made the first step—acceptance—and it is time for the second step."

"I mean help with those creatures out there," Bove swung his arm in an arc taking in the whole outside, "How do I deal with them?"

"Creatures? You don't *deal* with them; they deal with you as best they can. Like most animals, they are curious. Keep to the path and you will be fine."

"Yeah, great! What do you mean about keeping to the path?"

"You focus on the wrong thing, Bove. You must commit to your redemption. You must commit to taking steps to redeem yourself for your actions."

"Tell me what I am to do about those animals."

"You do nothing. You stay on the path to redemption, and all will be fine."

"And if I don't?" Bove challenged.

"Then you will die," Tanka stated.

"I've already reached the second hill and the path back is closed, so what will happen if I don't stay the path; if I go my own way?"

"You look much better than when I first saw

you. Do you feel better; I'm sure you do. You see your redemption will heal you, but only if you follow through to the end of the path. If you fail to follow the path all will be lost, and you will have to pay with your life for your decisions. That is not what we want or what you want. You know that, or you would not have accepted the errors in your decisions."

"I don't even know where this path leads or where it ends. And with the eagle and Cave Lion and whatever else is out there, I may not even make it to the end, and if I do what's there for me? I'll be redeemed and still in this awful world? What do I do then? Wait until someone happens by to get me off?"

"You must have faith the path leads home, and all will be well. Once you complete the road you will be free to move on—no longer in the turmoil of indecision. But first, you must complete your redemption. You have accepted the errors in your decisions, now you must commit to not make those same errors. Commitment is crucial to your redemption, it is the step that will elicit action, and action is what will make you whole. Commitment is the step you must take to proceed to the next hill. To commit is to swear to us you will not let the will of others influence your decisions. You must be true to what is right. Can you do that?"

"What?"

"Can you commit?"

Bove stared at Tanka, thoughts flying through his head. *I will have to believe in the right decision and not let others sway me. How am I supposed to know what the right decision is? Visions? Intuition? How will I possibly know that? How can I commit to such a thing?*

"I cannot commit to that," he said. "How can I know when to decide colonization is not right, and if I decide to go against the team the company will remove me. I won't be allowed on any expedition again, so what good will that be?"

"Making the right decision is not restricted to the colonization of new worlds; it involves any situation you find yourself in. You will be faced with decisions all your life and making the correct decision will be your commitment. Can you do that?"

"Yeah, I guess," Bove said shaking his head.

"You must be sure."

"Yeah, I guess, I'm sure."

Tanka studied Bove's face looking deep into his eyes for a long moment, then said, "Good, you can continue. Come, drink, and be rested for the remainder of your journey." He held out a cup of water and sat on the bench opposite Bove. He smiled and motioned Bove to him.

Bove hesitated long enough to take a deep breath and stepped to Tanka taking the cup and drinking the cool water. He sat on the bench a short way from Tanka at a loss for words.

"Step to the path to see where you are going. The sun has reached its zenith, so you must continue."

Bove glanced out the doorway, and turned back, "Tanka…," he started, then not seeing him, he thought *Gone, as usual. Gone and I have no answers.* Little choice remained. There was no going back, nothing to go back to. So, the only option was to continue to the next WayGate. *I guess I have committed to something— to redeem myself, but how?* he wondered.

He took another drink from the fountain and stepped to the doorway. In the distance were snowcapped mountains bordering a grassy plain. To the left were tall trees and what looked like a river below the bluff. And to the right was the first hill with its rocky sides hiding the bog in the distance. The third hill was hidden behind the TempleGate, yet it loomed in his mind as an obstacle to overcome.

He sighed and took a step out of the doorway committing to the next phase of his journey of redemption. A slight chill ran up his spine and down his arms, he felt a bit off-balance, then it was gone as if a spider had raced over him. He felt a slight dizziness before his head cleared. There was something he was thinking about, but he was unable to recall what it was, *oh well,* he thought and proceeded.

The path curved to the left and disappeared around the hill. As he rounded the curve, he could see there were no WayGates and no rest until the bottom. Small bushes covered the hillside, none large enough to provide much shade. His foot felt much better, and his arm was no longer hurting. It was awkward with the casts even though the one on his arm was half broken. He thought it was not doing much good in holding his arm in place, yet he did not want to remove it completely.

Why he was thinking of redemption he was not sure and wondered where that idea came from. Was he feeling guilty about his assignment on Kryth and not having told anyone of his visions? Or was he feeling bad about getting in a fight? Getting drunk and in a fight was not very smart, considering where it got him.

He kept a watchful eye out for the eagle and the Cave Lion and to his relief, there was no sign of either. He fell into a steady pace toward the WayGate at the bottom of the hill letting his mind drift over the events of the last couple of days yet having no recollection of what happened in the TempleGate.

The mission, the visions, and the final decision to not reveal them poked at his mind. Would it have made a difference if he had spoken up? Doubtful, the team had decided to recommend colonization and he did not have any hard evidence to disagree, so what would have been the point? *How can decisions be made on fantasies*, he wondered. And yet his visions seemed to have been more real than he thought.

He stopped to rest, once again his leg was starting to hurt but this time it was more his calf muscles than the ankle bones. Downhill travel put stress on his legs he was not used to, and with the cast, he was thinking his ankle bones should be hurting, not his muscles. And his arm was feeling fine, no pain, but there was no strain either. *Good*, he thought. *If this keeps up, I will be fine.*

He could see the WayGate below and the closer he came to it the more the third hill was blocked by the trees until he could no longer see it.

Fifteen

The WayGate was a relief and when he entered, the heat from the sun slid away. The stone bench was a welcome sight and he dropped down on it stretching his leg to ease the tight muscles. The walk down the hill had not caused any pain in his arm and only his leg muscles hurt. *Unusual*, he thought, *with breaks and fractures there should be more pain in the bones.* But the thought was dismissed and replaced with happiness.

The midday sun was taking its toll on his strength. *Rest*, he thought, *that's what I need, a long, quiet rest.* Taking a deep breath, he laid his head against the wall to clear his mind. But thoughts of his situation drifted to him. *I'm going to need shelter, food, and water either for the short term or longer if there is no rescue at the end of this path. And a weapon.* The encounter with the giant eagle had made him aware of the dangers on this planet and how they could injure or kill him, so yes, a weapon was needed, and soon.

He raised his head blinking at the fountain in the center of the gate. A long drink and splashing water on his face and through his hair made him feel better. He closed his eyes letting the coolness work its way into his body. He felt he could fall asleep for hours, but there was an urgency pushing at him—*do not rest long, the end of the path must be reached before sunset.*

He opened his eyes and gazed around the WayGate. It was like the other gates, murals covering the walls showing the forest of tall trees reaching hundreds of meters in the air, and the people working to build shelters in the tops of the trees. Walkways connected huts along the branches large enough to allow two to three people to pass. Small units for individuals and larger ones for meeting places were visible in the foliage. No activity was evident on the ground below where once these people had lived before ascending to the trees. Bove did not know why but wondered what caused the change.

Again, he laid his head back to rest before continuing his journey, and after a moment he looked out the exit at the path leading to the third hill. It curved into the foliage a short way from the WayGate cutting off his view. *Oh well*, he thought, *no choice but to proceed*. He stepped out of the WayGate onto the path.

It was easy going for a while—trees covered the path with shade keeping the air cool and comfortable. Shortly after leaving, he found the path blocked by a fallen tree at least two and a half meters in diameter—much too high to climb over. He stopped. The trees creaked with the slight breeze, the leaves rustled, and the hairs on Bove's arms stood up like a miniature forest. There was no way he could get over the fallen tree, but he could go around. *It couldn't be far around,* his eyes searched toward the base that remained hidden in the dense foliage. *A couple of minutes and I'll be back on course* he considered as he stepped off the path following the fallen trunk.

He worked his way through the undergrowth poking his walking stick ahead to be sure there were no surprises hidden in the bushes. Not much there except fallen leaves and a few small bushes-- nothing to worry about.

The tree was bigger than he realized. *A meter or two is all it should be,* he thought as he followed the trunk seeing no end to it. Ten or twelve meters from the path he came to the stump. It must have been hit by lightning causing it to break and fall. *Finally*, he thought, *I can get around it and back to the path.*

As he circled it, he heard a low growl to his left. He froze! His mind filed through animals that could make those sounds and came up with all manner of creatures.

He stopped breathing, muscles tightened, and his head turned back and forth searching for the source of the growl. He stopped when he saw the Cave Lion step from behind a nearby tree.

It was as tall as Bove with a massive chest and powerful legs ending in huge paws and sharp claws pressing into the soft loam of the forest floor. Its head was lowered showing a tuff of curly hair on its back standing up in anger. Two long canines protruded from its upper jaw and its nose wrinkled with each sniff of its prey. Its ears flicked forward then lay back against its head while two green eyes bore into Bove considering its next meal.

Sweat broke out on Bove's forehead and a shiver ran along his arms—his legs felt like they had grown into the forest floor, he couldn't make them move.

The Cave Lion stepped from behind the tree as Bove watched its muscles ripple across its broad shoulders. Its back tapered down to its hips and into its tail that swished slowly back and forth. It licked its jaws and dropped its eyebrows as it focused on Bove.

A chill ran through Bove from his back to his arms stopping at his hands gripping his staff with white knuckles. His mind ran through options. Run? Not good, the beast would be on him in a flash. Attack? No, he would not stand a chance. Stand his ground and wait to be dinner? No. Ease away slowly? Maybe. What is it they say about facing a wild animal—make a lot of noise and try to appear larger? Yeah, that's it!

In the instant for those thoughts to flash through his mind, he made his decision. He stood as straight and tall as he could, spun his staff around, and dropped it into a horizontal position pointing directly at the Cave Lion. He yelled, "Back!" and thrust his staff at his adversary then took a couple of steps back towards the path.

The Cave Lion growled stepped back and stared directly at Bove, eyes level with Bove's. Bove thrush the walking stick again, "Back!" he yelled and stepped back wanting to turn and run yet knowing he would not get two steps before the beast would have him.

The Cave Lion stood its ground and watched as Bove took another step back toward the path. *Even if I make it to the path there is nowhere to hide*, Bove thought. Keeping an eye on the Cave Lion he tried to devise a plan to defend himself; nothing came. He took another step back, *slow, and easy*. There was not even a tree he could climb, *even if there was the Cave Lion could climb it too,* he needed another option.

Suddenly the Cave Lion roared exposing fifteen-centimeter incisors then came at him snarling and snapping its jaws. Bove pushed his staff directly toward it with a quick jab and pulled it back before the lion hit it with a massive claw that swished through the air. It stopped and surveyed Bove a moment, its tail swishing slowing back and forth. Bove stepped back again and glanced behind him for some protection, he saw none.

The Cave Lion let out a low rumbling growl and attacked moving fast to the side of Bove's staff then lunging for him. Bove shifted to his right and banged into the tree trunk; while at the same time he swung his staff with all his might whacking the Cave Lion on the side of the head hard enough to startle it. He swung again from the opposite direction hitting the other side of its head. He took three or four steps back toward the path while the Cave Lion paused to regain its bearings. Another roar came as the Cave Lion charged again. Bove stepped back twice, stumbled over a branch, and crashed to the ground on his back. The Cave Lion pounced landing with its paws on either side of Bove and its fangs ready for a final atrocious bite to Bove's throat.

All Bove saw were two large yellowish incisors, wet with saliva and ready to rip into him. *This is the end*, he thought, yet he felt his staff lying across his chest and had no intention of giving in to this beast. Gripping the staff with both hands—and thinking his left arm is going to be shattered—he thrush it up and into the Cave Lion's open month where it bit closed, snapping the staff in two while jerking its head back. At that instant, Bove took the piece in his right hand and with every ounce of energy in his body whacked the Cave Lion on the side of its head, then again bringing his arm back and connecting to the other side of its head.

The Cave Lion whimpered and stepped back, shaking its head to clear it. Bove rolled onto his stomach and pushed himself up with his good arm. He lunged toward the path not caring if his leg hurt or how his arm was. He needed to get someplace to protect himself, but where, he did not know.

He was closer to the path than he realized and fell face-first onto it. *Great*, he thought, *I'm done, that beast will have me!* Nothing happened! He rolled over onto his back in time to see the Cave Lion disappear into the trees.

His whole body shook, his breath was coming in short gasps and his heart was pounding so hard he thought it would burst from his chest or explode inside of him. He took a deep breath to calm himself, then another letting the air out slowly as he felt his heart slow. He raised his short staff, pointing it in the direction of the Cave Lion while he tried to gain his footing—not easy with a cast on his left arm and a short staff in his right hand, but he managed. His legs shook, and he felt like he was going to drop back to the ground; he grabbed the tree trunk blocking the path and thanked the powers that he was safe. He looked at the broken staff and tossed the pieces aside.

He took two more deep breaths and tightened all his muscles for an instant. He relaxed and took another deep breath. The shaking calmed; his heart slowed. He was ready to get to the third hill and away from the Cave Lion. Twice he checked to the right and left of the path to assure himself there were no more threats from Cave Lions or eagles, and when he saw nothing, he breathed easier calming his frayed nerves and easing his stressed muscles.

How far, he wondered as he stepped forward to the next WayGate. The path turned a few meters ahead, obscuring the view of anything except trees. A chill ran through his arms and across his back and settled in his gut where it felt like a string had pulled his stomach back to his spine. He took another slow deliberate breath. His leg and arm did not feel any worse after the encounter with the Cave Lion, which surprised him, but he did not expect it to last.

The cast on his arm was falling apart even with the shoestring tied around it. He was thinking it may be as well to remove it altogether—he could get another. His leg also felt much better. *That's different*, he thought. His arm and leg should have a great deal of pain; he felt as if he was unhurt, although his heart continued to race.

He hurried along the path toward the WayGate keeping a watchful eye out for the Cave Lion to the right and left of the path. Tension slipped from his back and shoulders with each step and when he rounded a curve in the path, he saw the WayGate and thought, *Safe for now.*

Sixteen

The WayGate like all the others had carvings of various sorts of animals from small beaver-like mammals to large dragon-like reptiles on the outer walls. The inner walls were covered with a forest of tall trees with large birds in the sky above and smaller mammals on the forest floor, monkeys, and small birds in the forest canopy. The mural covered all the walls and the ceiling displaying a sky of bright blue with eagles soaring over the forest.

A fountain stood in the center of the gate and stone benches, onto which Bove sank with a sigh, lined the walls. *After this hill where will I be,* he thought, *on the other side and no closer to home. I have to get over this hill because that's where the path leads, and I have no other option but to follow it. Maybe there's a village or town at the end. Some civilization to help me. Going off the path would be foolish, and I would end up lost. No, following the path is the best option.*

He opened his eyes, knowing he could not rest long. He had to keep it together for one more hill. He glanced around the WayGate, noting the fountain at its center and the exit opposite where he sat. He pushed himself up from the bench, stepped to the fountain, and drank deeply of the cool clear water. He rested his hands on the fountain's edge letting the water soak into his body filling him with energy and vitality. He felt new again, reborn in a way, full of energy to keep him going on to the next hill. He stepped to the exit and considered the path ahead, it curved right, and halfway up the hill, he could see a CrossGate then the path circled the hill out of sight. It seemed less steep than the paths up the previous hills and was a welcome sight. He glanced back into the WayGate noting the absence of the entrance, then stepped out onto the path. The sun was hidden behind the hill, yet it cast light on the hillside before the CrossGate where he knew the temperature would rise. *Should enjoy the shade while it lasts*, he thought and headed up the path.

It was smooth and level with a low slope making it easy to ascend, and shortly he was at the CrossGate. It was a cool spot after coming into the hot sunlight and he sat with his leg on the stone bench wondering why it only had a slight ache, and his arm was feeling normal. He thought he could remove the cast with no dire effects but chose not to. *Better leave it on until I can get it checked,* he thought. Feeling regenerated he went up the rest of the hill.

He was able to see the TempleGate above although the path seemed to disappear around the top of the hill. *Will this temple have some answers? A note or a sign to let me know I'm not abandoned on this rock. Someone has got to be waiting for me and this temple is it, I'm sure of it.* He took a deep breath of the dry air and wished for a breeze to cool the heat from the sun.

As he proceeded, a second CrossGate came into view indicating the path looped around and crossed itself twice. *That's why it is easier to go up,* he thought, smiling to himself.

He passed through the CrossGate and was soon

entering the TempleGate at the top of the third hill. It was like the other temples, larger than the other gates, and the outer walls were decorated with carvings of lions, monkeys, bears, and wolves. Birds of various kinds soared above other animals. The inner walls were adorned with murals of the forest and its people settled in the village high in the treetops. The stone floor was cool and in the center was a fountain with cool clear water bubbling up in a spout.

He stepped to the fountain and drank deeply to clear his head. It had been hot with the sun beating on him as he made the walk to the temple. His injured limbs were not hurting like they should be. He was fatigued from the walk. *Strange*, he thought as he drank more of the refreshing water.

"You have arrived at the TempleGate of Action."

The voice caused Bove to jerk up from the fountain. He turned; Tanka stood across the temple close to the exit. He wore a robe of dark maroon that shifted from a bright red to pink, it shimmered as he moved giving the impression of a red sea flowing in and out like the tide.

"You are at the final temple," Tanka said. "This is the Temple of Action, where you must decide if you are to be redeemed or forever cursed to the follies of your actions. If you choose to continue you will be bound by the choices you make here and now."

Bove felt a slight lightheadedness, a bit of a shifting in his mind; he knew he had spoken to Tanka in the other temples, and the memory of his commitments was clear.

"Choices, I thought I had already made all the choices I needed to. What more must I do?" he asked.

"You have committed to accept you made the wrong choice when you failed to tell of your visions, and you have committed to making the right choice in the future whatever the situation. You must commit to *acting* when an injustice is committed. That is your final step toward redemption. Can you commit to that?"

"To speak up when I see something wrong? Yeah, I guess so."

"No, to do what must be done to stop the injustice. Can you commit to that?"

"Yeah, I guess so. I accept I should have told of my visions initially in the debrief, but even if I did it would have been unimportant, the decision had already been made, and my input would have been irrelevant. So what good would it have been to tell of the visions?"

"It is not about the visions you were given on Kryth. You must accept that in future situations you must act. You were given information you could have used to protect the people of Kryth, but you chose to ignore it. You made the decision to let the people of Kryth be destroyed with the colonization of the planet, is that not true? So, in the future, you will be in situations of similar nature on which you must act. You must do the right thing when you find yourself facing such a decision. If you decide to do the right thing, that will be good. But, if you choose to take the easy course, you will pay the consequences. This is the action you must commit to; the action you must take to redeem yourself. Is that clear?"

"What do you mean by acting on it? Will I get more visions and I'm supposed to act on them?" Bove looked at Tanka with disbelief in his eyes. "And what if I decide not to? What are you going to do to me? What can you do to me? Granted you can give me visions, but in the end, they don't change anything. They don't affect the physical world, so I can do nothing and have no ill effects. And as for your redemption..."

"My redemption?" Tanka's eyes flared in anger as he stepped close to Bove. "It is your redemption of which we speak! It is you who has ignored the warnings; you who have put our people in great danger; you decided your own pleasure is more important than the lives of others. It is you who needs to be redeemed! You have been given a great gift; a vision of the future; a vision that tells you what must be done to preserve precious life, and you will choose to ignore it. You will choose to let those suppressed be taken advantage of?" Tanka dropped onto the bench against the walls of the temple and signed, "I thought you were better than this, I thought you would accept to change the outcome when possible, but I see I am wrong. Unfortunate."

Bove looked at Tanka not sure what to say.

Tanka looked up, studying Bove for an instant then continued. "If you decide to not commit to take action when needed your only choice is to remain here."

"Remain here? In a vision? I will wake from and find myself on the Mars?"

"Oh, you misunderstand. As was explained to you before, you are both here and there, and there can be terminated at any time. We do not have to let you return to your reality. Only through redemption can you be granted that option. As you see the only way out of this TempleGate is back from where you came," Tanka said, gesturing to the entrance through which Bove entered. It was open, and outside, the path led to the bog, clearly visible in the sunlight.

Bove fell to the bench, dazed. The gravity of his

situation hit home! He thought he had some control; some say in the outcome only to find how mistaken he was. It seemed his only option was to commit to act, to do what he must to get back to his ship. It is not right for someone to have such control over others, no matter what has been done. Everyone should have the right to decide how to handle their own life, how to use the information provided, and make the decision they think is right. No one should be able to dictate the actions of others. It is not right.

"What must I do?" Bove asked defeated, "And how do I know if I will return to my ship?"

"You must believe your actions will make a difference and act. Believe you can affect the outcome of a given situation, be it the decision to colonize a world or to steal a can of beans, either is wrong and you must do what is needed to prevent it. Can you do that?

"What exactly are you saying? I must step in when I see something wrong or voice my disapproval?"

"Oh, you must intervene to stop any action of that nature. You must protect those whose rights are being abused. You understand what you have done by ignoring the visions you were given?"

Bove nodded.

"You understand. You must act on any knowledge you receive involving another being violated. That is what you are committing to, and you will do so until your redemption is completed."

"I see," Bove let that sit in his head while he considered. "And when will the redemption be completed?"

"Come, drink, and be rested for the remainder of your journey." Tanka held out a cup of water and sat on the bench opposite Bove. He smiled and motioned

Bove to him.

"You didn't answer my question," Bove said.

"There is no answer. Redemption is a process, not an action. You are redeemed when you are redeemed, and only you will know when that is. All we can offer is the path to redemption."

"Offer it? You dictate I must take the path; I must do as you request. I have no other option. So, if I were to decide my redemption is completed now, will I have fulfilled your request?"

"Do you feel you are redeemed? Do you feel you have satisfied your inner conflicts over not telling of your visions when they would have had the most impact? Do you feel you are free of any guilt for the destruction of a civilization? Do you feel there is nothing else you can do to help anyone in a similar situation? Is that what you are feeling? If so, you have taken the first step to redemption, but you will not be relieved from committing to help when it is necessary. That will be your burden and what you must accept. Redemption is an ongoing process of making the right decision for someone in peril, not once but in every case. You must commit to doing that."

"And that commitment is my only option?"

"No, you can decide to remain here."

"Like I said it's my only option since I will not stay here. What must I do to show I have committed?"

"You will show your commitment in decisions you make in the future. We will help you with visions and guidance when needed. You will not be alone."

Great, Bove thought. *Just what I need, a nursemaid looking over my shoulder.* Then he said, "So I am free to continue to the end of the path?"

"You are," Tanka answered.

Seventeen

Bove looked toward the far side of the temple to see the exit no longer covered with a mural. He turned to bid Tanka farewell only to find him gone. *Okay*, Bove thought, *Now I can get back to the ship*. He stepped to the fountain to quell his thirst then walked out the doorway into the sunlight where he felt the warmth fill his desire to be home. Again, his mind shifted causing a slight dizziness, his thoughts cleared. *When will I get to a place where I can be picked up? No one around to help just this path; oh, someone is going to pay once I'm back on the ship. If I get back.*

He stopped a meter from the TempleGate and scanned the view. To the left, the path turned, went through the CrossGate, around the hillside, reappeared on his right, and ended at the base of the hill in a WayGate. Across the plain, he could make out the next WayGate sitting on the edge of a bluff that seemed to drop down. To what Bove could only imagine. *Is that the way back?* he wondered.

The downward trip took only a few minutes as he circled the hill crossing the path twice as he had while ascending, and soon reached the bottom WayGate where he could sit and catch his breath. His arm and leg were feeling normal, and he considered removing the casts to make moving easier but decided on the side of caution. He looked out the WayGate exit to gauge the distance to the next gate which was visible across a flat area of small Joshua trees—one to two meters high. Short sawgrass covered the ground between the Joshua trees. The gate sat only forty to fifty meters away. *Simple*, Bove thought, *a short walk with no interference. A shuttle should be waiting just over the bluff.*

He stepped out of the WayGate into the afternoon sun. The air was heavy and pressed against him like a thick blanket pressing on him. He felt like taking a long nap even though he knew he had to keep going. The only way to return to the ship was to continue forward. *But why*, he wondered, *was there a shuttle waiting for him?* If so, how was he to know, there had been no communication since he woke, no indication anyone was aware he was here, so why did he have to keep following the path? Something kept pushing him to keep going, to stay on the path to be redeemed.

The path was clear until he was about halfway to the next WayGate, where a large rock sat right in the middle of it but did not appear to extend much on either side. He stopped and considered the best route around.

To the right were a couple of Joshua trees not impeding the way, and to the left were a few rocks, smaller than the one blocking the path and they too were not an impediment. Bove chose the left figuring he could climb over the rocks if there were more he could not see.

He stepped off the path to the left and headed around the rock, and as he approached the backside he heard a soft growl, more a purr than a threat yet a shiver ran up his spine as memories of his encounter with the

Cave Lion flooded his mind. His shoulders tightened, and his heart raced. He peered around the edge of the rock expecting to come face to face with the Cave Lion. He relaxed when he saw it was not there and let the tension slide from his shoulders.

He glanced around and spotted the Cave Lion less than twenty meters away. It was lying on the ground, paws crossed and a drowsy look on its face. Yet when Bove made eye contact with it, its ears lay back on its head, and its eyes opened and focused directly on him. It rose to its feet and flicked its ears forward.

Bove stepped back behind the rock and back on the path. *It's far enough away I should be able to get around the rock and with luck to the next gate,* he thought hoping to convince himself it was possible. It was his only hope of a safe place, and what other options did he have?

He checked to the right of the rock hoping to slip around and head to the WayGate. As he stepped off the path the Eagle sailed over his head made a quick turn and dropped to the ground, not thirty meters from where he stood. The muscles in his stomach tightened, adrenalin flooded him, and his hand curled into a fist wishing he still had his staff.

The eagle will not be as quick as the Cave Lion and with luck, I can make it to the gate before the Cave Lion realizes where I am. Also, I can use the trees for cover. I will make it, he thought as he bolted from behind the rock for the nearest tree. He found he was wrong on both counts. The eagle was in the air and halfway to him before he reached the tree, and as he glanced to his left, he saw the Cave Lion bounding at full speed toward him. Fear pushed him toward the tree knowing he would never make it.

Before he reached the tree, the eagle was on top of him. Its beak was open, and its claws were ready to rip into him. He dropped to the ground and rolled to the left hoping to avoid those sharp talons. Before the eagle's beak clamped shut on him the Cave Lion plowed into it. The eagle screeched and tumbled to the side as the Cave Lion bit its wing.

Bove scrambled to his feet and headed for the WayGate. A slight pain ran up his leg, not enough to stop him from moving forward. The eagle screeched again and leaped into the air as the Cave Lion howled and leaped after it, missing its wing by a hair's breadth.

Bove came to the path again and glanced back over his shoulder to be sure he was not being pursued. The Cave Lion was after the eagle leaping into the air trying to reach it, but the eagle stayed out of reach of it. The path curved away from the WayGate and a straight line would put him there sooner. He turned off the path for the shorter distance to the WayGate and the eagle swerved in the air and headed toward him, dropping to his level. The Cave Lion bounded after it, roaring as it approached. Bove leaped to a small tree for shelter near the WayGate. He rolled to the backside as the eagle dropped towards him. The Cave Lion leaped for the eagle's throat with a piercing yelp. Bove held his breath and pulled into a ball against the tree trunk.

There was a screech from the eagle and the tree shook, limbs fell on him, and he saw the eagle with the Cave Lion gripping its shoulder fly away and disappear. Their screeches and roars faded into the snapping of trees and crashing of rocks tumbling down the hillside.

Bove let out his breath, glanced around, and listened for any sign of either of them. There was only silence. He stood and looked toward the WayGate, then to his right and left—nothing. He wiped the sweat from his forehead and stepped out from under the tree. His legs felt weak, his heart pounded, and his hands shook. He took a deep breath and rubbed his eyes.

What the hell, he thought.

Feeling the danger had passed he rapidly headed for the WayGate, arriving with no further incident. He stepped into the cool of the gate and dropped to the stone bench with a great sigh of relief. Several deep breaths helped slow his heart as he lay his head against the stone wall. Feeling safe eased the tension in his shoulders and neck and his body relaxed.

Eighteen

After several minutes he roused himself to his feet and thought about what was left to do. *Follow the path and you shall arrive home,* he wondered why that was so, then put it aside, *so let's get on with it.* He took a long drink from the fountain in the center of the gate before going to the exit.

Before him was the bluff leading to a river below. It was covered with small sage bushes and rocks with a small Joshua tree here and there. Below, tall White Oak trees crowded the riverbank. The bodies of the Cave Lion and the eagle lay among the stones next to the path, neither was moving. The path switched back on itself about halfway to the river and the eagle lay above the switchback while the Cave Lion lay below it. Bove didn't trust they were dead, so he cautiously watched both as he proceeded down.

He saw no indication of movement from either body, and as he made his way past them both, he felt the tension slowly leave his shoulders. He thought of inspecting the bodies but decided it was best to continue to get back to the ship. *It can't be much farther,* he thought.

The remainder of the trip to the riverbank was uneventful and at the bottom of the bluff, he entered the shade of the trees. The sun was getting low in the sky and the air was cooling. The shade was a wonderful relief from the heat of the day. The path disappeared into the darkness of the trees and Bove stopped and studied the way ahead. Slowly his eyes adjusted to the dark shadows, thick trunks of the trees and small bushes clustered along the riverbank. The sound of rushing water came off the river flowing next to the path and the air felt thicker yet cooler.

Bove shrugged the coolness off, and before proceeding, wondered what was hidden in the trees. His visibility was only ten to twelve meters through the foliage, and he thought up all manner of monsters lurking in the shadows. He shivered from the musty air and proceeded. The path narrowed and became rough with tree roots bulging through the ground and rocks poking up making walking slow. Little sunlight reached the ground making the forest dark and colorless. The smell of damp earth filled his sinus making breathing slow and broken.

He stumbled over roots and banged his cast on protruding rocks, cracking it, while continuing to move forward. *This is the final leg of this journey,* he thought, stepping over another root.

There was a rustle in the underbrush to his right causing him to freeze and listen carefully. It came again, loud like a large animal of some kind. He stood his ground and the noise moved closer, then suddenly a great bear-like creature stood up out of the underbrush only a couple of meters from where he stood. His breath caught in his throat, his shoulders tensed, and his heartbeat against his chest like a wild animal trying to escape from within. The creature was two and a half meters of thick fur, massive shoulders, and arms ending in four-fingered paws with sharp claws. Its head was shaped like a bear with a shorter snout, a wide mouth with long teeth, and two small sinister brown eyes that bore into Bove. It was the beast Bove had seen carved on the outer walls of the WayGate.

It roared bearing its sharp teeth and flinging spittle in Bove's face. It spread its arms out two meters on each side but did not approach.

Bove extended his palms forward, fingers spread while backing along the path. "I mean no harm," he said softly taking another step back that put him off the path.

The creature roared and dropped to all fours, then with a push, it charged. Bove turned, stepped back onto the path, and headed quickly away. The roar stopped and all became silent. He stopped and slowly turned back stretching his arms out stiff with fright.

"Easy," he said glancing back. The beast stood still, shook its head, sniffed the air towards Bove, turned, and ambled off into the forest.

Bove stood quietly for several minutes listening for it to return, letting his muscles relax and his heart slow. There was no sign of it and after a couple of minutes he turned and headed down the path, faster than before.

The path continued through the dark shadows of the forest and the river bubbled its presents, revealing no gate. He felt like he had been walking for hours with no change other than roots and different bushes. The path continued in deep shadow and seemed to get darker as the minutes slipped by.

Shortly, he heard falling water, like a waterfall, a short way ahead. Hope soared at the thought of a change. He continued until the waterfall was loud and near. He pushed on, soon stepping into a small clearing.

At the far end, a waterfall rose thirty meters in dark shadows. The sun was behind the top of the hill, light sparkling through the top of the falls. The water was crashing down in a roar and a mist spread over the grass covering the clearing where a TempleGate stood. It was much larger than the others, yet of the same design and covered with the same carvings as the other temples.

Bove approached it anticipating the end of his journey and a way back to the ship. He hurried to the entry and stepped in. The interior was void of the fountain found in the other temples and there was no bench to rest on. The far wall was covered with curtains of green and red flowers on a light blue background. The rest of the walls were decorated with murals of trees with animals below and birds of many colors flying above the treetops and sitting on branches. The dome showed a sky with scattered clouds.

Bove glanced over the murals and then focused on the curtains on the opposite wall. There was no apparent exit. He stepped to the center of the room searching for a doorway out to get him back to the ship.

"You have made it to the final temple," Tanka said.

Bove jerked around to see Tanka standing to his right close to the wall and their conversations came flooding back to him. He remembered the three temples and the conversations in each with Tanka. He remembered the commitments he had made. It all seemed so clear, so right.

"Yes," Bove answered. "I see this is all an illusion, a dream. I only have to wake."

"That is not true. If you could awake from this, wouldn't you have done it already? Or if so, do it now.

Awake!"

Bove stepped back trying to wake, trying to break the dream, or vision, or spell, with no success.

"You see," Tanka said, "this is not a dream. It is as it was; you are both here and there. Where to return is still open."

"Open?" Bove asked. "I've done everything you asked. I've committed to your redemption. What more is there to do?"

"You must believe," Tanka said. "Come, rest after your journey. You must be tired." He indicated a soft couch next to him.

"Tell me how to get back to the ship," Bove said sinking into the couch.

"Rest," Tanka said, "all will be as it should. Lay back ease your muscles and let your thoughts drift. Relax."

Bove sat, feeling how tired he was, he lay back relaxing his muscles and easing the slight pain in his arm and leg. His eyes slid closed, and his thoughts drifted. He was in a room with little light and across the room was a figure sitting facing him. The figure reached up and a lantern flared to life, casting light through the darkness, and sitting looking at Bove was Kabluff.

"There are things you must know," Kabluff said.

Kabluff, Bove thought, *from Kryth, from my visions...*

"Yes," Kabluff said. "From Kryth and here to guide you to your future."

"My future?" Bove asked.

"You have committed to do the right thing as you go forward. In the future, you will be faced with a critical decision affecting the future. Because of your decision on Kryth, things have been put into motion that will change things in the future, and you will be faced with a decision determining the outcome. Your decision will determine if the future falls into chaos or remains stable.

Kabluff watched Bove absorb this, then continued, "That is why you were given the chance to redeem yourself for the mistake you made when returning from Kryth. And you have committed to do the right thing, and when the time comes you must make the right decision."

"Yes," Bove said bewildered, "I will make the right decision…"

"You see the need for redemption. Why you have committed." Kabluff reached out and touched Bove's shoulder.

Bove jerked awake at the touch of his hand. He sat up to get his bearings, looking for Kabluff but someone pushed him back down.

"Agent Sandle," a voice said. "Please stay still."

"What…"

"Stay still you've broken your casts."

"What…"

Your casts, on your arm and leg, were broken and I had to remove them. What kind of a dream did you have?"

"Dream?" Bove wondered aloud. "What do you mean *a dream*?"

"Please, don't move or you may damage your arm and foot. Your casts need to be replaced. The bones won't heal correctly if they are not held in place."

"My arm and foot?" They didn't hurt, or even feel sore. Yeah, he had casts on them a while ago, he has long since healed. And how did he get back on the ship? Bove closed his eyes and rubbed his forehead wondering what had happened.

"The doctor will be in shortly and we will get those casts replaced," the nurse said.

"But nothing is wrong with my arm or foot," Bove insisted, "They feel fine."

"Yes, I'm sure they do, but let the doctor decide." The nurse pushed back the curtain circling the bed and peered out for the doctor. "Yes," she said. "He's coming now."

Bove rubbed his eyes as Doctor Travis stepped through the curtains. *Another vision,* Bove thought.

"Well, what have you been up to, breaking your casts like that," the doctor asked, not a question. "You could damage your arm and foot more. Did you have a bad dream?" He bent over Bove and studied his arm then looked over his foot in as much detail.

"We better get some new scans to be sure there's no additional damage, okay?" Turning to the nurse he said, "Can you get the scanner." He turned back to Bove as she nodded and left, "Let me check those limbs."

The doctor picked up Bove's left arm and felt along the wrist to the elbow, "Any pain?" he asked.

"No," Bove tightened his fist and twisted his arm. "No, no pain at all."

"Strange," the Doctor mumbled reaching for Bove's right ankle. He felt around the ankle squeezing slightly, "and here?" he asked.

"No, none there either."

"How about your chest? Your eye seems to have cleared up. There's no bruising or swelling. Quite remarkable."

"The chest is fine," Bove rubbed his chest and took a deep breath.

The nurse returned with the scanner and handed it to the doctor who nodded to her. "Okay, let's see what we have."

Doctor Travis scanned Bove's arm from the wrist to his shoulder, twice. Stepped back and looked at the scanner, set it down, and picked up his tablet. He tapped it a few times, picked up the scanner, and looked at it again. He turned to the nurse, "Get me another scanner this one seems to be on the fritz."

The nurse disappeared through the curtain.

"Is the scanner broken?" Bove asked.

Doctor Travis nodded and stepped to the side of Bove's bed. "Seems to be. Look here," he said turning the tablet toward Bove. These are the scans of your arm and foot I took last night when you were admitted. They clearly show fractures in your left talus and your radius. These don't heal in a day, usually more like six to eight weeks."

The nurse returned with a new scanner and the doctor repeated the procedure on Bove's arm, ankle, and ribs with the same results. "Interesting," he said and once again turned the tablet toward Bove. "It seems your arm, ankle, and ribs are no longer injured. See the scans I just completed? They show no signs of fractures on any bones. I don't know what to tell you."

Doctor Travis looked at the scanner again and tried another scan. Up Bove's arm, around his ankle, and over his chest, and checking the results he found the same thing—no fractures. "I am puzzled. This is very strange, very strange indeed."

"Can I get out of here?" Bove asked.

"I guess so. I see no reason to keep you any

longer. Although I would like to run some additional tests, so stay available for the next few days."

"Right, where am I going to go?"

*   *   *

Bove left and headed for his cabin wondering what had happened. How could he have healed so quickly? Was the vision/dream real, a real experience? Had he repeated the experience from the planet? Were those commitments he made real? He would have to sleep on it. *Things will look better tomorrow.*

Once he arrived at his cabin, he was feeling a little better. He was back in a familiar place, his cabin, and back on the Mars heading home. He sat on his bed, stretched his arms and legs out, and closed his eyes tightening his muscles and taking a deep breath. There was no pain, only tiredness.

"You have done well," Tanka said.

Bove snapped open his eyes and there stood Tanka

"What are you doing here?" Bove asked bewildered.

"Following up," Tanka said, "Just following up. You have returned whole, unharmed, and wiser. Remember your vision and your commitments; that is the path you have chosen to follow." He nodded to Bove, "I must go." He said and left.

Bove jumped to the door. "Wait!" he said following Tanka into an empty corridor. He was not surprised that Tanka was gone, he stepped back to his bunk and dropped onto it.

What now? he wondered. *I can't continue to have visions on assignments. I can't stand against the company and expect to continue with First Encounters. What now?*

He lay back, closing his eyes. *What now?* he wondered.

Part Three
Ibex

Nineteen

The smell of beer and fried food permeated the stale air in the dim light of The Pilot's Pub where a waitress cleared one of the tables while Ben, the bartender, wiped the bar. A few customers were finishing their lunch while talking quietly among themselves. It was a typical Tuesday afternoon at the lunch stop for workers from the United Planets Space Port across the road.

Bove leaned back in his chair and took a sip of his third Jack Daniels and ginger ale as he thought about the last three months. His search for work had always ended with the look, the creasing of the forehead, and a second glance at the resume, which said everything. *Well, we'll keep you in mind...*, and so on. It was the First Encounter experience that worried them, why was he no longer part of the elite force, the team that forged the future of mankind, the best of the best? Something had to be off, something that would make him wrong for any position. That's what hung in the air after each short interview, though never spoken it was clear what they thought.

Every day he spent looking ended at The Pilot's Pub where he drown his failure in liquor.

The muffled sound of ships launching reminded him of the times he had left the spaceport on a new adventure to find new worlds to colonize. He finished his third drink and ordered another. The first Encounter Teams—a division of the Galactic Peacekeeper Force—launched all their missions from the spaceport. Five years he had reported for duty to seek new planets for the great expansion into space. The Manifest Destiny defined the current government's determination to dominate the galaxy, at whatever cost. Bove had been a part of that until he had the visions. Visions of events put into motion by his agreement to colonize the Delta planet of Phoenix-Gamma. Events that massacred the indigenous life of that planet to make way for mankind's expansion into the galaxy. The visions forced him to repent for his lack of action against colonization. All that led to being assigned to desk work, something Bove could not tolerate and did not accept, so he resigned and now found himself out of work and depressed.

After the vision of the three hills, he had to tell someone, so he went to the ship's psychologist. Everything was supposed to be confidential, but the next day he was called into the mission commander's office and asked what he had experienced. He tried to explain and convince the mission commander he was not affected by his vision and that he could still perform his job, but the commander was not convinced by Bove's story. So he consulted with the psychologist and together they decided Bove could best serve on desk duty until he was better. What *better* meant was anyone's guess.

A tear ran down his face as he thought of what the visions had shown him of the inhabitants of the planet Kryth. *Kryth, no it was the Delta Planet of Phoenix-Gamma, that was the official name, the name everyone used.* But he knew better, or did he? Were the visions real? No! They were only disturbances in the mind, as the psychologist had told him. Fantasies of his thoughts; but he had been there in the vision and saw the planet destroyed; laid to waste by the invasion. And he had walked the path to redemption over the three hills. Yes, he had experienced all of it, if not in real-time but in virtual time, and it was real to him. That was why he was no longer considered a good prospect for First Encounters—he was compromised!

They told him there would be a review every six months to evaluate his condition and if he recovered his perspective he may be fit for duty. That meant he would be on desk duty the rest of his career, that he had flown his last mission. He couldn't accept that. The First Encounter Team and their missions were what he lived for and without that, there was no point in his staying. He resigned from the Peacekeeping Force and now had to deal with that decision. He drank to dull his pain of failure.

He knew it was not the way to success, but he couldn't help himself. He was turned down at every opportunity and it seemed pointless to hope anything would change. He was ready to take any job to earn some credits, even something temporary. But even temporary work was not available. He took a sip of his drink letting the cool liquid slip down his throat as he tipped his head back and gazed at the ceiling.

Ben slid a chair out across from Bove and sat. He studied Bove for a moment, then tapped the table with his knuckles. Bove was lost within himself. Ben tapped the table again and cleared his throat. Bove glanced down, blinked, and shoved his chair back, "What do you want?" He blinked again, "I've paid my tab…"

"No. You haven't, but that's not the point." Ben gave Bove a chance to focus on his words, then said, "You interested in work?" He straightened up, studying Bove for a reaction.

"Huh," Bove tried to focus.

"I said, are you interested in work?"

"Yeah." Bove gazed at Ben not sure what he was asking.

"I have someone looking for a pilot. You interested?"

Bove's mind began to clear, he thought he heard right, there was a job, but was it anything worth his while? He thought not, yet he needed something. The prestige of the First Encounter Team drifted through his mind saying he was too high valued for just anything. There was respect when he had returned from a mission, people were there to greet him, to show him how important he was, how he had played a part in the mission to expand the influence of the human race, to make us superior, and rulers of the galaxy. To fulfill the Manifest Destiny of populating the galaxy, they cheered his part, but now there was no cheering, only rejection, and he needed work.

"Bove," Ben cut into his thoughts. "Are you okay?"

"Huh?" Bove said shaking his head. "What'd you want?"

"I have someone that wants a pilot and you seem to need some work." Ben reached over and pushed Bove's shoulder. "Your tab is more than I should carry, so you should talk to this guy."

Bove shook his head and looked up at Ben. "What does he want?" he asked.

"A pilot," Ben repeated.

Bove shook his head again. "A pilot for what?" he asked.

"I don't know. He just said he needed a pilot. He wanted to know if I knew anyone. I told him I'd check. So, do you want to talk to him?"

"Yeah. I'll talk to him." Bove pushed his drink away.

"It's kinda urgent. He's back there." Ben pointed to a table at the back of the bar.

"What's his name?"

"Don't know. Don't care. Go talk to him." Ben stood pushing the chair under the table.

He looked down at Bove, a flicker of concern crossing his face, and pointed to the back of the room. "There, at the back table. You need to go now." He reached out and touched Bove on the shoulder, slightly gripping him. "You need the work."

Bove glanced back toward the table, then looked at Ben again. "Okay," he said. "I'll see what it's about." He stood and realized he was drunker than he thought. He took a deep breath, nodded to Ben, and made his way to the back of the bar.

He slid into the seat and studied the man across from him. He had dark skin with curly brown hair falling around his face, his brown eyes pierced Bove with intensity, his mouth was a tight line of seriousness. "You okay?" His eyes searched Bove's face.

Bove nodded.

"I need a pilot and I hear you are one of the best. That true?" He fixed onto Bove's eyes looking deep into them as if seeing into his soul.

Bove flinched, then nodded.

"You don't look so good. Are you sure you can

handle a starship?"

Surprise lit up Bove's face. "A starship?" He pulled himself straighter in his chair.

"Yeah. Is that a problem?"

Bove shook his head, took another deep breath, and tightened his arms and legs trying to clear his fogged mind. "What kind?" he asked.

"It's a class two freighter. Ben said you're former First Encounter. That true?"

"Yeah. What's the job?"

"Why aren't you with the First Encounter anymore?"

"I quit."

"Why? That's a pretty good gig. Why would you quit?"

"Personal reasons." Bove glanced around the bar and shifted into a new position in his chair.

"Personal huh? Are you hurt? Frightened? Burned out?"

"I said it was personal. What's the job you have?"

The man leaned back a frown creasing his brow. "I've got a package to deliver and I'm running late. It pays five hundred credits—a hundred when you show up tomorrow and the rest when the package is delivered. Can you handle that?"

"Five hundred, huh?"

"Yeah. Can you handle it?"

"Yeah, I can handle it. How long's it going to take?"

"A week, maybe two."

"Is this a one-time thing?" Bove asked hoping for a *No* answer. "If you don't have a pilot could you use a permanent one?" He tried to look sober.

"Maybe. You want the job? I don't have a lot of time"

Bove straightened in his chair and took a breath. "Yeah, I'll do it. When do we leave?"

"Tomorrow six AM at launch bay 46B. You're sure about this?"

"The ship?"

"Yeah, the ship, the job. Can you handle it?"

"I can fly anything. This won't be a problem."

"I hope you're right. If there're any problems, you won't be happy."

"Six AM, 46B—tomorrow. I'll be there."

"Be on time and be sober."

Bove nodded then watched as the man stood to leave. "What's your name?"

"Lucus, and you?"

"Bove."

Lucus nodded and walked out.

Bove wondered what he had just agreed to. Something didn't feel right. Lucus seemed edgy, anxious about his package, and desperate to get it delivered. A chill ran up Bove's spine and he crossed his arms over his chest to ward it off. *Too much to drink,* he thought laying his head on the table.

Twenty

Bove stood in the concourse reading the sign for launch bays 40-50. Passengers hurried past on their way to their flights, each pulling a suitcase behind them and carrying an extra bag over their shoulder. Unlike domestic airline flights, which were never more than a day, a trip to the stars could take a week or two, or longer. Changes of clothes, materials for work and relaxation, and personal items were needed in their cabins.

Bove adjusted his bag on his shoulder, shifted his backpack, and scanned the bay numbers for Bay 46B—it was toward the end of the concourse. He made his way avoiding other travelers who crowded past him in their rush to make their flights. He remembered the times he would rush for a flight with the First Encounter Team. Always ready for the next adventure on some new undiscovered planet. Excitement had run high during his first flights, but as time went by, the thrill receded with the days slipping into the past until the great adventure had become a job, much like any other.

He shrugged the memories away and pushed through the door to Launch Bay 46B. In the center of the bay sat a starship. The ship was large with the bridge sitting on top of a protrusion like the neck of a turtle. Below the bridge was a flat window of an observation room. On either side at the front was a blaster. Behind the protrusion was a support platform supporting two cargo bays. Nestled between the cargo bay and the ship's fuselage was a blaster—one on each side. The ship's engines were below the support platform between the cargo bays, and on top of the platform was a box-like structure with "IBEX" displayed on its side in faded black letters. The entire ship was battleship gray and looked in fairly good condition.

Not much of a ship, he thought. *Probably only needs a crew of six or seven to run it.* He walked around to the rear looking it over to get a feel for its shape and handling capabilities when he ran into Lucus.

"You made it." Lucus closed a folder in his hand and tucked it under his arm.

"Did you think I wouldn't?"

"The last guy I hired didn't. You're here so let's get started." He waved Bove to follow him.

The loading bay door was open creating a wide ramp into the cargo hold. Lucus went up the ramp with Bove close behind. At the top of the ramp was the loading bay, it was empty. To one side in storage racks were a couple of tractor lifts, next to them were a couple of utility lifters, all securely held in place with clamps. Several EVA suits were secured in transparent containers next to the lifters.

At the back of the loading bay was a cargo holding area where the cargo was sorted and checked before moving it to the hold in the front two-thirds of the deck. The cargo hold was closed off from the holding area by a three-panel door—two panels that slid in from the sides closing off the sides and the lower half of the opening. The third panel slid down from the top fitting into the flattened "V" shape left by the side doors. Next to the loading door was a common door for easy access. This was a standard setup for cargo ships.

There were three doors in the holding area, two marked Docking Port and Shuttle Bay. The third was unmarked but it obviously led to a corridor toward the main body of the ship. Bove made note of the layout, particularly the single entry to the cargo hold which seemed secured.

Lucus headed straight for the door leading to the main ship. "Deck six is the main entrance to the ship," he said. "But since everyone's already on board we should find some of the crew on deck three or four. You can meet them." He stopped at the end of the corridor waiting for Bove to catch up. Bove stepped into the main body of the ship where another door, marked *Cargo Bay B,* led to the other cargo bay. Next to that door was another marked "Airlock" and across from it, was a lift. Next to the lift was a stairwell.

"Are both bays the same?" Bove asked.

"Yeah," Lucus said. "You can check out bay A, but B has sensitive cargo." He pushed the activate button for the lift and when the door slid open he stepped in motioning Bove to follow. They exited at deck four.

Deck four was a long corridor that ran the length of the ship. Lucus pointed out the medical unit, recreation room, fitness center, dining room, kitchen, and storage rooms for everyday items. At the front end of the deck was a stairwell that led up to deck three where the crew quarters were.

"Wait here." Lucus stepped across the corridor into the dining room and shortly reappeared followed by one of the crew. He was about Bove's height and weight. He wore a pair of light gray casual pants with a matching pullover shirt. Black sneakers covered his feet making quiet steps. He had brown hair, almost blond, a sharp nose, a firm mouth, and gray eyes with tension lines at the corners.

"Meet Dan, our *Mister Know It All*. Dan knows everything there is to know about this ship from the engines to the weapons. He knows how they operate and how to fix anything when it goes wrong. We cannot do without Dan."

"Good to meet you." He nodded to Bove.

"Likewise."

Lucus grinned and patted Dan on the back. "Come on and meet the others."

Stepping from the lift onto deck three Bove spotted a short dark-haired woman coming out of one of the rooms lining the corridor.

"Aw, Lucy," Lucus said bowing slightly.

Lucy stopped in front of them, her eyes shifted to Bove, looking him up and down with a slight smile on her lips. Bove shifted from one foot to the other and stepped back from her. He moved his gaze from her bright brown eyes and oval face quickly scanning her delightfully curved and soft-looking form; an attraction that tensed his muscles.

"You're the new pilot?" She asked locking her eyes on his.

"Uh yeah." Bove blinked.

"Yes," Lucus interjected. "Bove is our new pilot and quite a fine pilot. He is a former First Encounter pilot."

"First Encounter huh?" Dan interjected. "What happened?"

"Let's not get into that," Lucus said patting Dan on the back again. "Lucy is our computer expert. She knows everything about the computers that run this ship,"

"Okay," Bove said nodding to Lucy.

Seven cabins lined the corridor, three on each side of the main corridor and one at the end. "These three," Lucus said pointing to three doors, "are empty. You can have your pick."

"I'm in the one at the end." Dan pointed to the door at the end of the corridor.

Bove glanced around the corridor noting the stairwell next to the lift, "Do the stairs run through all decks?" He nodded towards it.

"Yeah," Lucus said. "From the bridge to the cargo deck. But there's nothing down there but crates— you know cargo. You can check out cargo bay A if you would like to see a bunch of crates. Cargo B is the same—no need to look at both."

"Anything down there I need to know about? You know to keep from damaging it during travel?"

"Nothing you need to be concerned about. Tom takes care of the cargo; you just pilot the ship and things will be fine." Lucus studied Bove, his eyes never leaving Bove's face, and then he turned and nodded towards the cabins. "Take your pick."

Bove took the first empty one on the left. He entered to find the cabin large enough for a bed, a desk, and a small bathroom. Storage units built in the walls had room for hanging clothes and drawers for non-hangers. Bove tossed his bag and backpack on the bunk. "Nice," he said.

"Okay, now to the bridge," Lucus said after Bove returned to the corridor. He proceeded to the lift to go up to the bridge. Bove followed with Lucy and Dan close behind.

"You'll spend most of your time on the bridge. Of course, you'll have time to sleep and eat, but we have a deadline that can't be missed, so that will be your focus." Lucus pressed the activate button for the bridge and the door quietly closed.

"You ever flown a ship like this?" Lucy asked.

"Not this specifically, but I've trained on almost every ship built, including this one. It's not much different from a lot of others. It'll be a treat to fly it."

"Well," Lucus said. "We'll see just how well you do. I'm already behind schedule and have a day to make up. My client is expecting delivery in a week."

"Where?" Bove asked.

"Ceti-2 in the Tau Ceti system."

"And you want to make that in a week?"

"No, I want you to make it in a week."

"Ceti-2. It'll be close. It'll take three, maybe four, days to get there once we're in the system. And it's three days from here to a transit point."

"Shouldn't be a problem if you're as good as you claim."

"We can make Ceti-2 in three days. If we run into problems, well I can't say. Could take longer."

"Well for your sake it better not," Lucus' voice was low and threatening, "This package is very important, make no mistake."

Bove felt a pricking on the back of his neck in the close quarters of the lift. Lucus' bulk seemed to press against him as he moved back touching the wall. The door opened and he followed everyone out into deck one.

He started to say something to Lucus when

Lucy interrupted. "The bridge is just at the end of the corridor; Jack should be there. You'll like him, he's a heck of a guy."

"Shall we?" Lucus extended an arm toward the bridge.

Bove followed everyone forward wondering what that was all about. Lucy didn't want him asking Lucus questions, and Lucus was expecting Bove to do what he told him, and that didn't sit well. Bove contemplated that as they approached the bridge and he decided to keep to himself, for now. There was always later to ask about things, like why was this package so important, and why did Lucy not want a confrontation between him and Lucus. And why had he taken this job...

"So, here's the bridge, your new home." Everyone followed Lucus onto the bridge. It was a standard setup with the pilot and navigator side by side facing the main view screen. To the right was the systems console for monitoring the ship's status, next to that was another array of instruments for monitoring the cargo bays. On the left was an array of instruments for monitoring the computers that controlled everything on the ship. That was Lucy's station. Behind the pilot and navigator on a raised platform was the captain's seat. The higher seat allowed a full view of the bridge and all stations, as well as an unrestricted view of the main screen.

Dan stepped to the consoles on the right and took a seat.

The equipment was standard and appeared to be the original equipment that came with the ship. No upgrades. Bove had been trained on these systems but never expected to see them in a ship. Lucy was responsible for maintaining them, which meant she was quite talented in computer system technology. These systems were mostly out of date and needed a good understanding of the internals to maintain them. Lucy had to know every detail, unlike newer ships that ran themselves. *Interesting*, Bove thought.

"And this is Jack our navigator. He'll get you anywhere you need to go, and I mean anywhere." Lucus said.

Jack turned from the console and looked at Bove scanning him from head to foot then rose to greet him. Jack was a couple of inches taller than Bove. He had chestnut brown hair and a Roman nose, full lips, and brown eyes that displayed no emotion. "You're our new pilot?" He didn't offer his hand or any other welcome, like a smile or nod. "Take a seat there," he pointed to the seat on the left facing the main viewer. "We leave in fifteen minutes. I was wondering if you would make it after what Lucus told us last night."

"Last night?" Bove turned to Lucus.

"Nothing," Lucus spoke up. "Nothing at all. You were a bit under the weather, and I thought you might oversleep is all."

"Well, I didn't." Bove took his seat at the pilot's console. An array of instruments covered the panel in front of him. He scanned the controls to familiarize himself with their function.

"Just as well," Jack glanced at Bove. "Like I said we leave in fifteen minutes, so you had better get ready to launch."

Lucus sat in the captain's chair overlooking the bridge. "You'll have to meet Tom after we launch. He's probably in the hold making sure everything is secure."

"Right." Bove ran his fingers over the controls

to get a feel, then he started preparing everything for the launch. There were checks to run, settings to be made and the crew to inform of the pending launch.

Bove checked the trajectory off Earth to verify the positions of the moon and the other planets. Once free of Earth's gravity they would accelerate to one-sixteenth light speed; they would reach a transit point in just over three days. Bove thought the ship wouldn't hold up at a higher velocity,

The path he laid out was straight from the earth to the Oort Cloud and flying at an angle to the solar plain they would be clear of asteroids and comets which lay mostly on the solar plain.

"Systems check." Bove turned to Lucy for a report.

"Systems are a go." She glanced back from her console and caught Bove's eye, gave a quick nod, and a slight smile curved her lips.

"Cargo status," Bove asked.

"Loading-bay ramp raised and locked, and the cargo is stable and secure." Came the answer.

"Airlock docking bay, and shuttle bay status?" Bove set the launch count-down.

"Secure, secure, and secure," Dan stated.

Bove switched his communication to the launch Bay Control room. "Open Bay 46B doors for launch."

"Bay 46B doors opening. One minute to secure open."

"Copy that." Bove switched to internal communications. "Launch in five minutes. Everyone buckle down." He checked the engine status then announced. "Engines primed and holding on stand-by."

Launching from a planet was simple, they only had to reach escape velocity to be on their way, but once free of gravity, everything changed. The acceleration was quick so there were dampers to counteract the force of the increase in speed, otherwise, everyone on the ship would be flattened against their seats. The force pressing against them would exceed what the human body could survive. Everyone would be crushed to death. So, it was critical that the dampeners were working before launching. Once they reached cursing speed the ship's artificial gravity would activate allowing the crew to move normally.

"Damper control status?" He asked.

"Dampers set to engage with acceleration," Lucy answered.

The remaining time slipped by quickly and Bove's console alerted him to the thirty-second mark.

"Thirty seconds to launch," he announced then checked the launch status. His console gave a general display of all systems on the ship—no detail only *go* or *no-go* status, and everything was showing a green *go* status.

"Five seconds. Everyone secure?" He didn't expect an answer. Everyone was responsible for securing themselves.

"Two seconds," Bove flipped the launch button cover. "One," He ran his left hand through his hair, said, "launch." Then pressed the button.

The launch was like every other launch Bove had experienced. The pressure was extreme for the first minute or so, then it disappeared, and he was weightless pressing against the safety belt that held him in place. The ship had reached escape velocity in under a minute and was flying away from Earth.

Suddenly the ship began a rapid acceleration to cruising speed and the dampeners engaged. The sensation was like someone pushed you back then immediately pulled you forward again. Then everything was normal. After acceleration, the artificial gravity engaged, and everyone settled into their seats. Now the crew could move about normally.

Post-launch system checks were reported to the captain. The ship was on course and would reach cursing speed in three hours. All systems were working properly with no abnormalities.

Bove let out a breath to release tension and leaned back in his seat. It would be three days before they reached the edge of the Sol system where they could transit to the Tau-Ceti system and during that time they would be traveling at one-sixteenth of light speed. It was the transit from here to there using entangled particles that made the trip to Tau-Ceti so quick, but that had to wait until they were clear of any bodies—planets, asteroids, or debris of any kind.

In the meantime, Bove was free to learn about his new assignment aboard the starship Ibex.

Twenty-One

Bove stood up after verifying everything was set for the trip to the system's edge. Acceleration was proceeding on schedule and Jack was checking the course. Everything looked good. "We're three days from transit." Bove turned to Lucus. "Am I needed for anything else?"

Lucus glanced up, "Yeah," he said. "We have a welcome dinner planned this evening. It's not every day we get a new crew member, so Dan will be cooking up something to celebrate your joining the crew. Six o'clock in the dining room." He glanced at Bove, nodded, and said, "Nice launch. Get settled in," then looked back at the console in front of him.

Bove nodded. Turning to leave he noticed Lucy was not at her console and Jack was busy checking coordinates for the transit point. The rest of the bridge was empty. Facing the exit, he noticed a doorway to the left of the main entrance. *The captain's office,* he wondered. He stepped out from the bridge, and he looked down the corridor as the bridge door slid closed. He ignored the lift and stairwell next to the bridge entrance and walked toward the rear of the ship noting the labels on each door, Electrical Equipment, Spare Parts, Servers, Weapons Control, and at the end of the corridor, Armory. Next to the armory door was a digital lock. He made a mental note. *Never hurts to know where the weapons are,* he mused running a hand through his hair. On their way to the bridge, Lucus had skipped decks two and five, so Bove decided to see for himself what was there.

To the right of the lift when Bove stepped out onto deck two were two doors—the conference room on the right and Captain's Quarters on the left. Knowing Lucus was still on the bridge Bove tried the door to the captain's quarters. It was locked.

Behind him toward the front of the ship was a double door labeled "Observation Conservatory," it was unlocked. The room was enormous with a huge window covering the entire forward wall. Unlike the view screen on the bridge, this was a window looking to the front of the ship. A black field dotted with stars covered it. In front were several tables and chairs, and behind those were a line of seats where a single man sat. His blond head faced the observation window. Bove could tell he was tall, two or three inches taller than himself.

"Hi," Bove said to the back of his head.

The man glanced over his shoulder at Bove then raised a hand as he looked back toward the window.

"I'm the new pilot." Bove tried again to start a conversation.

"Yeah, I know." He continued gazing at the window not acknowledging Bove in any way.

"You must be Tom," Bove ventured.

"Yip."

"What is it you do?" Bove asked.

"You ask a lot of questions," Tom said turning his blue eyes at Bove. He studied Bove for a moment, then turned back to the window.

"Not really, that was the first actually. I figure

we're going to be together for a while and I want to get to know the people I'll be working with.

"So now you've met me," Tom said keeping his back toward Bove. A clear message that he was not interested in any conversation.

Bove sat next to him and looked out at the stars. They seemed so peaceful, quietly glowing in the dark sky, yet beneath that clam was a torrent of activity that could destroy a world with a flash of a flare. That was the feeling Bove got from the crew, an undercurrent of dissatisfaction rippling through the ship. He couldn't put his finger on it, but it was there in the background, in everyone's attitude except Lucus'. He seemed okay with the mission.

Tom turned to Bove, "Just what are you after?" He asked.

"Nothing really, I just getting to know the ship and the crew…"

"That so?"

"Yeah, I like to know the people I work with and the job we're doing."

"Don't worry about the job. You just get us there and back. That's all." Tom studied Bove for a second then turned away again.

"So I heard." Bove could feel the tension from Tom, ignoring it he continued. "The thing is, I like to know why I'm hired to do things and what it is I'm doing. You know in case I've gotten into something illegal."

Tom snapped around towards Bove. "What are you saying? You don't trust Lucus and in turn, me?" His eyes flared, his jaw tensed, and his hands gripped the arms of the chair. He pushed himself to his feet and took a few steps away from Bove. He turned back and his voice raised, "Who do you think you are?" He glared at Bove. "You were hired to fly us there and back and that's all you need to know. If you have questions, ask Lucus." He spun around and sat at one of the tables, back to Bove.

"What are we delivering?" Bove stared at Tom's back.

"You don't need to know." Tom didn't move. "Drop it."

"Okay," Bove studied Tom for a moment, stood, then headed out for the lift feeling uneasy. He considered the mission, unknown purpose, and package. Tom wasn't revealing anything. *Must be because I'm new,* Bove thought, *or is it more?*

He considered what he knew. Lucus and Tom knew what was being delivered, he didn't know about the others, but maybe they knew too. But no one seemed to want to talk about it. Everyone knew where they were going—Ceti-2—but no one mentioned who they were meeting. So, they were going to Ceti-2 to meet someone and deliver something. Bove needed to know more.

He stepped out of the lift on deck three and headed for his cabin. Lucy's cabin was next to his. Tom and Jack were in two of the others, but Bove didn't know which. Dan was in the one at the end of the corridor. Bove took some time to settle in, putting what few items he had into drawers and his toiletries, toothbrush, razor, etc. in the small bathroom. He had no pictures to hang or personal items like gifts or memoirs. His parents were long gone, and he had no siblings or girlfriend, in fact, no friends at all. He was alone and had been since he had joined the First Encounter Team five years ago. There wasn't time to make friends while he worked for the Corporation, only time to explore and rest between missions.

It was only in the last three months that he had time to himself and all he had done with that was brood about his lack of work and his lack of purpose or meaning. He felt lost in a world where he didn't belong, a world of ordinary people who did ordinary things like date, make a living, socialize...live. A world that didn't want him, that rejected him at each opportunity, denied him work, and why? Because of the visions, because he had told of them and their consequences because he had threatened to stop the colonization, the great move forward because he had cared. Cared about the lives of the inhabitants and not the credits to be made from the colonization so he was pushed out to a desk job, a job where he would die of boredom if he remained, so he had quit.

Now he had a chance to live again and not to have to deal with visions or missions, or bureaucrats wanting what they wanted no matter the cost. He was free to do what he wished. Except he had to deal with this mission and the undercurrent of dissatisfaction that prevailed throughout the ship. He needed to find out what was going on—why everything was such a secret and how it was going to affect this job. A job that was starting to look like a single trip. He couldn't suppress the unease that once the package was delivered, he would no longer be needed. He would again be looking for work.

He bumped into Lucy outside his cabin and reached out to grab her before she fell.

"Geez, watch where you're going." She pushed away from him.

"Sorry." Bove let go of her shoulders.

"You should be," she stepped back straightening her clothes. She glanced down, rubbed her shoulders, and looked up again. "You hungry?"

"Uh, yeah." Bove's stomach growled in protest to only a slice of toast and coffee since morning.

"Okay," Lucy said, "Do you know where the kitchen is?"

"Yeah, Lucus showed me this morning."

"We don't have a cook, so everyone fins for themselves unless someone feels cookery—like Dan-- and makes a meal for us."

"Like dinner tonight?"

"Yeah, like dinner tonight." Lucy glanced at him, "Come on."

Bove knew where the kitchen was, but there hadn't been time to check it out when he was with Lucus earlier. Inside was a dining area with six or seven tables, a partition with an opening and door that led into the cooking area, where there were stoves and ovens, a freezer, and in the back were pantries holding all the dry goods. Everything latched and locked to prevent things from floating around during zero gravity. Even inside the cabinets, items were secured in place.

"Okay, so this is the kitchen." Bove glanced around taking in the layout.

"Yeah," Lucy looked around. "And this is where you will find everything you need to survive." She smiled, leaned against the counter, and looked at Bove, "Can you cook?"

"Not much, I do get by though."

"Okay, let's see what you can do." She opened the freezer and pulled out some meat, then the refrigerator and the pantry setting everything on the counter. "Make something," she said.

Bove shook his head; he had never cooked anything other than frozen meals. He looked at all the stuff sitting on the counter. "I don't make stuff, I heat it."

"Then you will learn." She proceeded to take pans, pots, and utensils out from drawers and cupboards lining the walls. She defrosted the meat and then started to mix items putting water on the stove to heat, and pans with oil to warm meats and vegetables, once everything was cooking, she turned to Bove, "See it's not so hard, and you need to know how to do this, or you are going to be eating dry bread and water."

"Okay," Bove shrugged. "So, what is this dinner about?"

"Oh, Lucus just likes to welcome new crew members with something."

"He does this for everyone?"

"Yeah, or lunch." Lucy stirred the food cooking on the stove.

That sounded too casual, like Lucy was avoiding talking about it, or maybe it was just lunch or dinner. But Bove didn't get that feeling, there was something else going on, like Tom's quick jump to anger when Bove mentioned doing something illegal. And Jack's dismissal when they met like he didn't want to get friendly. And other than Lucy, Dan seemed the only one accepting Bove. It didn't feel right.

"Let's eat." Lucy spooned food into the dishes and pointed to the outer room. "Let me serve you."

Bove retreated to the dining room, selected a table, and sat down.

Lucy brought plates of food out and sat them before him. "Enjoy," she smiled unconvincingly and sat across from him.

*   *   *

After eating, Lucy gave Bove a tour of the rest of deck four. The Fitness Center was equipped with muscle-building machines—arm and leg development for both front and back muscles—triceps, biceps, calf, and thigh. There were machines for back and abdomen muscle building. Cardiovascular machines, treadmills, stair-stepping, rowing, and stationary bikes. There were monitors for blood pressure, heart rate, bone density, and fat content.

Even with artificial gravity, it was vital to maintain your physical body in good shape. Bove was glad to see all the equipment and eager to use it.

The recreation room had a screen covering the back wall for showing movies of which there were thousands stored in the computer archives—according to Lucy. She offered to select one for Bove's pleasure. He declined.

In the forward section of the room were game tables including a pool/ping-pong table, a fizzball table, and a card table. Cabinets held other games to entertain the crew. Each game was on a memory chip that when inserted into the gaming table displayed a virtual game.

At the back of the deck were a couple of storage rooms for supplies. What was in them wasn't mentioned. Another mystery.

The medical center was equipped for minor injuries and diagnosis of illnesses, but not to treat anything. There was no doctor or medic to treat medical issues. If they were to have an event causing injury or sickness there was no one to treat them—not a good situation. The cabinets contained medicines to elevate pain and treat infections. They could only hope for an event-free trip. Bove didn't ask about the lack of medical personnel but figured Lucus had his reasons.

The afternoon seemed to pass quickly and Bove was ready for dinner when Lucy had finished her tour of the deck. They took the lift back to the crew quarters saying they would see each other at dinner.

*　　　　*　　　　*

Bove was ten minutes early for dinner and thought about asking Lucy to go with him, but their afternoon was more of a tour explaining the ship than a friendly encounter. He took the lift to deck four and stepped into the dining area finding everyone there and seated around a group of the tables pushed together for the occasion. The table was set with the usual meal setup—plates, utensils, napkins, etc.—for each member of the crew; and at each place was a glass filled with wine.

Lucus sat at the end facing the door with Tom and Lucy on his right. On his left side were Dan and Jack.

Lucus pointed to the chair at the foot of the table, "Please, have a seat."

Bove glanced around as he pulled the chair out and sat facing Lucus.

"So," Lucus started, "As everyone knows Bove is our new pilot. To welcome him I offer a toast," he raised his glass, "To our new pilot and a successful mission." Everyone clicked their glasses and took a drink. Lucus looked toward Bove, "So Bove, tell us about yourself."

Bove was a bit surprised and was at a loss for words momentarily. Regaining his composer he said, "Well there's not much to tell. As you know I was with the Galactic Peacekeeping Force before joining you. That's where I got my training as a pilot." He looked around the table and then took a sip of wine.

"You were with the First Encounter Team, right?" Tom asked.

"Yeah."

"How long?" Tom waited, watching Bove with narrowed eyes as if calculating his next remark.

"Five years." Bove took a bite of food and a sip of wine.

"You never told me what happened," Dan spoke up. "Why you left."

"I did," Bove glanced at him, "I told you it was personal."

"Well," Tom said, "That's kind of vague, don't you think."

"Tom," Lucus said, "If Bove wants to tell us why he left he will, I'm sure."

Tom turned to Lucus and started to say something, paused, then said, "Yeah, I guess."

"I did a little research," Dan said, "And it seemed there were some issues with your last mission, but I couldn't find any details. Only that there was controversy about the mission. Were you involved with that?"

"No." Bove leaned back in his chair and took a breath. "Look, I have my reasons for leaving the First Encounter Team. Reasons I don't want to discuss, so please drop this."

"Yes," Lucus said, "That's enough about why Bove left his prior employment. Tell us about your family."

Bove took another sip of wine, "Okay, I have no siblings and my parents died several years ago. That's about it." He looked around the table, "Can you tell me more about this job? What are we delivering and to who?"

There was silence as Tom glanced at Lucus. Lucy and Jack looked at each other and took a sip of their wine. Dan stared at Bove; mouth open as if to say something.

"Bove," Lucus started, "some of our clients are very particular about their cargo, and themselves. They prefer to remain anonymous as to their identification and their business. This job is like that, so in respect of our client, who they are, and what their cargo is, is on a need-to-know basis."

"Is it legal?" Bove asked.

"Of course, it's legal. We don't participate in illegal activities. Do we Tom," Lucus stared at Bove, eyes deadly serious.

"No, of course not," Tom said glancing around the table as if to tell everyone to keep quiet. They did.

"Dan," Lucus said, "let's have dinner."

Dan nodded and stood up, then looked at Lucy and asked, "Will you help?"

"Sure," she answered.

They disappeared into the cooking area and quickly returned carrying dinner. They sat bowls of vegetables, meat, and bread on the table. Once everything was ready, they sat down and quietly waited.

During all this, Lucus talked with Tom in a faint voice that Bove could not hear. Jack leaned toward Bove asking if he had settled in okay, if he had any questions about the ship, etc.

Lucus looked up at Bove, then turned to Dan, "This looks great. Proceed."

"Ok," Dan said picking up one of the bowls of food and handing it to Lucus. The food made its way around the table as everyone served themselves.

"So," Lucus looked at Bove, "no family. What about friends?"

"Work has kept me pretty busy the last few years," Bove commented. "What about the rest of the crew," he said. "Jack, where are you from?"

That opened conversation concerning each of the crew. Everyone freely told Bove where they were from and about their experience and how they came to be part of the crew. Everyone except Tom, who remained quiet the whole time watching Bove.

Lucus had turned to his food and didn't participate in the conversation. So, at the end of dinner Bove knew about Dan, Jack, and Lucy, but nothing about Tom or Lucus. He thanked Lucus for the welcome dinner and headed out intending to get some sleep.

At the lift Lucy stepped in next to him and requested deck three, as the door slid shut, she spoke up, "You shouldn't have said anything about this job."

"Why not?"

"It's not in your best interest," she looked at him silently for a moment, "This isn't the best client to have."

"What do you mean?"

"I overheard Tom talking to Lucus about it and they mentioned a weapons dealer. Apparently, someone Tom doesn't want to be associated with, but Lucus has a package that must be delivered, and he's committed us to follow through."

"A weapons dealer?" A frown crossed Bove's forehead, that didn't sound good. As far as he knew, weapons dealers were ruthless and didn't like changes to the deals they made. This didn't sound good at all.

"Yeah, that's all I know." Lucy stepped out of

the lift and headed for her cabin.

Bove caught up to her, "What's the package?" he asked in a muffled voice in case someone was listening.

She turned to Bove, and took a step back anger clouded her face, "No one knows," she snapped.

"Okay," Bove raised his hands, palms out.

"Get some sleep," Lucy turned and headed for her cabin.

Twenty-Two

Bove woke to a soft charm followed by a female voice stating the time as six AM ship time. He rubbed his face pushing the night's slumber from his mind, and after a quick shower, he headed for deck four to get breakfast. Jack was there having instant eggs and toast. He looked up when Bove entered, "Morning," he said.

"Morning," Bove nodded looking for bread to toast.

"You work out in the morning?" Jack asked taking a bite.

"Huh?" Bove poured coffee into a cup still not fully awake and not knowing what he was going to do next.

"Exercise," Jack said.

"Yeah, I guess so."

"Two hours every morning keeps you in shape."

"I do one. Always have and I'm fine."

"Finish up and let's get to it."

"What's the push?" Bove was in no hurry to stress out his body this early in the morning.

"We need to talk. In private." Jack stood up. "Coming?"

"Yeah." Bove reluctantly followed taking a slice of bread and leaving his coffee. He wasn't going to pass up a chance to talk about whatever it was that Jack had in mind.

In the fitness center, Jack stepped onto a treadmill. "Everyone else works out after hours. I'm the only one that's here in the mornings so we won't be disturbed."

"So, why do we need privacy?" Bove started the treadmill next to Jack.

"You asked some delicate questions at dinner."

"About this job? Nobody wants to talk about it and it's making me uneasy."

"Leave it alone, Tom and Lucus are handling it, and Tom will make sure you stay out of it."

"Tom? He's Lucus' right-hand man, right?"

"Yeah, he keeps everyone in line. You don't want to cross him."

"I don't?"

"No."

"So, what are we delivering?"

"Don't know and don't care."

"You should. What if it's illegal? Dangerous? Something that could land you in prison. Lucy said we're delivering to an arms dealer. If that's true it could be illegal or dangerous, or both."

"Did you ask her where she heard that? Lucus hasn't said anything about who or what we're dealing with."

"Is she close with Lucus?"

"Nobody's close with Lucus except Tom." Jack stopped his treadmill, and turned to Bove, "Look, all I'm saying is leave it alone and stay out of Tom's way. After last night Tom's going to be watching you, and you don't need that. Just let Lucus take care of this and get us our credits."

"Credits, huh. How much?"

"Lucus didn't say, but it's more than we've seen before. Lucus says it will be our biggest payday."

"So you're in it for the credits?"

"We're all in it for the credits.

*   *   *

Bove spent the rest of the day reviewing the ship's procedures and functions. He studied the shuttle bay procedures memorizing the locking and unlocking of the shuttles and the bay layout. Any open airlock or shuttle door would prevent a shuttle launch, He studied both cargo bays. They had the same layout, and both had a corridor leading to the stairwell in the main body of the ship. The one difference was that cargo A had the shuttle bay while B had only storage. He reviewed the specifications for the engines, weapons, life support, and computer systems.

By the time he completed his review, it was time for bed. He was hungry and tired, too tired to bother with food. He ate an energy bar from his backpack and crawled into bed satisfied with his understanding of the ship and its functions.

*   *   *

Morning came early. They would reach the transit point in the afternoon, so he had time for a workout and breakfast which was needed after the long day before with little to eat. While going through his morning activities he thought about what he knew concerning the mission.

After talking to Jack and Lucy he was convinced they knew nothing other than their destination. Lucy had overheard Lucus and Tom mention the arms dealer, and he wondered why she hadn't told Jack or Dan, but none of them seemed to care what the package was or who was receiving it.

Their only concern was the credits, but no one said how much they would get. He was making five hundred and wondered how much the crew would get. *It must be considerably more*, he thought.

As he prepared for the bridge, he reviewed the tasks of the day. Transit procedures would have to be reviewed, with the older systems in the ship, it was going to take an hour or more of prep before doing the transit. Newer ships could do a transit with the celestial coordinates and a push of a button. His first task would be to verify their ETA to know when to start the preparations. He headed to the bridge.

Jack was there checking their position. Lucus sat in the captain's chair and looked up when Bove entered, "Looks like we are right on schedule and on target."

"Good," Bove sat in the left seat and touched the buttons to active his console. He checked their position, "Looks like we will be in position at 16:30."

"So military," Lucus said, "You can call it 4:30. How long will it take before we can transit?"

"About an hour. We'll start prep at three-thirty," Bove turned to Lucus, "If it takes longer, we will still be in the Tau-Ceti System today and on our way to Ceti-2. That will be a three-day trip leaving us two days to spare."

"Not quite," Lucus said, "a week was overstated. They are expecting delivery in three days, and we can't be late. Our client does not accept lateness."

"Why the change in the schedule?" Bove asked.

"Because our client wants that," Lucus said.

"That's cutting it close. If we run into problems, we'll be late."

"Not acceptable." Lucus glared at the back of Bove's head. "Get us there or you'll leave the ship without pay."

"What?"

"You heard me. The deal was to get us to the rendezvous point on time to make the delivery. If you don't do that I don't pay. Is that clear?"

"That's four hundred credits."

"Then get us there."

"We can't get a day's slack?"

"He won't give us an hour, so we need to be on our toes and make good time through the system. Got that?"

Bove nodded and turned back to his console to verify the data. "Jack, you know the protocol for a transit?"

"Yeah."

"And Lucy?"

"She knows. This isn't something new to us you know, we've done quite a few transits."

"It's you I wonder about," Lucus said. "You're the unknown here, so do you know the protocols?"

Bove turned back to Lucus, glanced at Jack, and saw Lucy enter the bridge, "What'd you think, Lucus? I'm a former First Encounter pilot. I know the protocols for every type of engine and have flown most. Yeah, I know what I'm doing."

Lucy slid into her seat and kept her head down studying her console.

"Okay," Lucus said. "We'll see…"

Bove stood up. "We need to be back here at 15:30 and ready to transit at 16:30. I'll see everyone then." He stormed off the bridge without looking back.

"16:30?" Lucy asked.

"4:30," Jack said, "Subtract 12."

"Huh?"

"Where's Dan?" Lucus asked.

      *   *   *

What the hell! Bove thought as he waited for the lift. *First, we have five days, now we have three. The trip out so far has been problem-free, but with this ship who knows want can happen*? He slammed his fist against the lift wall. The lift stopped and the door slid open to deck three.

What's going on? he wondered while stepping out and looking at the stairwell next to the lift. *What's down there?* Curiosity drifted through his mind, then he decided to check it out. He knew it was risky not knowing where Tom was, but if they were delivering something illegal, he needed to know. If the cargo was weapons, as he suspected, that would be trouble, and trouble was the last thing he wanted. No one had said the hold was off-limits, although Lucus had said their client, and their cargo, was confidential. *Well, I won't know what cargo is for this client, so what can it hurt?* A poor excuse, but he had to find out what they were shipping.

The corridor was empty as he slipped through the door to the stairs; Dan or Tom could be in their cabins and come out any time, or Tom could be in the hold. *It's now or never*, he thought heading down the stairs that ended on deck six in a small alcove with a single unlocked door. He carefully opened it and peeked out to see the small area where the cargo bay corridors ended. Next to the stairwell was the lift. Bove crossed to the door to cargo bay B and entered. The short corridor ended in the Bay holding area. From there a door opened to a short path leading between holding pens. A steel grid enclosed each pen with a locked gate. Inside each were crates strapped to the floors and walls; everything was held tightly in place to avoid movement during flight. The path turned to the right and extended halfway through the hold; more cargo cages were in view at the back of the bay. There was no movement and only the hum of the engines.

More storage, he thought stepping around the corner and heading farther into the hold. He followed the path looking into each pen to see creates of assorted sizes. Some labeled medical supplies, others labeled foods or distinct types of tools. Similar crates filled all the pens; all securely held in place.

He came to a branch leading to the right where he heard a woman's soft voice quietly singing to herself. Turning in the direction of the voice it became louder, then stopped. Bove also stopped and waited.

"Tom, is that you?" The woman said, "You're early, or have I lost track of time?" Then silence and a moment later. "Tom?"

Whoever was back there was expecting Tom, but why would there be a woman in the hold? Was she working with Tom? *Let's see what we have*, he thought and stepped to the end of the path to find another pen secured with a steel grate and a locked door. Behind the grate was a woman in a loosely fitting tan jumpsuit and a pair of utility shoes. Light brown hair framed a young face with high cheeks, a nose slightly curved up at the tip, full lips, and eyes matching her hair. Those eyes studied Bove with questions.

"Who are you?" she knotted her brow and glanced over his shoulder.

"I'm the pilot, Bove." He glanced back to see what she was looking at. "You were expecting Tom?"

"He brings my food three times a day and it's early for lunch," She wrinkled her brow, "What are you doing down here? I thought I was off-limits to the crew."

"Maybe, I don't know. No one told me not to come. Who are you, and why are you locked up down here?"

"You had better leave, if Tom catches you down here you're going to be in trouble."

"You didn't answer my question," Bove said.

"I'm Stella, now go."

"Why are you here?"

"I'm to be delivered to Zabi." She stopped as they both heard the hiss of the cargo hold door opening. "Quick get down in there and hide." She said pointing across the path. I'll hum and little tune when all is clear.

Bove stepped across the path and into the enclosure which luckily was unlocked. He crouched behind a large crate to wait. Shortly he heard Tom and Lucus talking as they approached and stopped at Stella's cage.

"Well, it looks like we are going to make our delivery, young lady," Lucus said. "Later today we'll transit to our location and then tomorrow we'll deliver you." There was a couple of seconds of silence, then again Lucus spoke. "It's been a pleasure having you onboard. I am sorry you couldn't enjoy more of the ship."

"Like you care," Stella said. "You're only interested in the credits. They'll kill me you know."

Bove peeked over the crate to watch. Lucus raised his hands, palms out like he was pushing something, then dropped them to his side. As his arms came down, he turned glancing around at the other cages. Bove quickly ducked down holding his breath.

"Oh, don't be so dramatic," Lucus turned back to Stella. "They only want information. Tell them what they want and I'm sure you will be on your way. Nevertheless, it's not really my concern. I'm only doing my job and my job is to deliver you to them, for a tidy sum I might add. Tom, you have our girl's lunch?"

"Yeah." Tom slid a tray of food under the door. "You'll get a special treat tomorrow before we turn you over. Kind of a farewell meal so you know it's not personal—just business." He glanced at Lucus then turned checking all around.

"You pig!" Stella yelled as they receded through the hold and out the door.

Bove came back out and stood in front of Stella's cell because that's what it was—a prison cell.

"So now you know why I'm here," she said. "Now leave before they come looking for you." She turned and went back behind some boxes that gave her a little privacy. Bove went back to the stairwell and headed to deck four where he entered the medical center. He had a lot on his mind, things were not as they had seemed, this was not just a delivery, it was human trafficking, but why?

Delivering Stella to an arms dealer was not what he had signed on for. It went against everything he believed and everything he had worked for. Life is not about the credits, particularly when it involves another person. Bargaining for a profit, obtaining a rare commodity worth a fortune, good old-fashioned work to achieve an end. That was what was meaningful. But people for credits—No!

He checked the medical panel for headache treatments. *The delivery*, came into his thoughts, *is to happen when we arrive. We don't have two days, we have tomorrow. And why are they giving Stella to this Zabi, an arms dealer?* Bove shook his head in bewilderment and scanned the next screen. The sound of the door sliding open alerted him that someone had entered.

"So, there you are," Tom said stopping next to Bove. "I've been looking for you."

Bove turned and looked up at Tom. "Yeah, why?"

Tom's piercing blue eyes studied Bove like he suspected something. "You know in a ship like this there are shipments that are private. Lucus told you that, remember?" He stepped closer to Bove. "Our clients prefer no one knows their business and we are committed to honor that. So, there is a restriction on anyone entering the cargo bay. You haven't been down there, have you?" His eyes held steady on Bove's, looking deep into them, watching, searching for something, waiting for a reaction.

"No," Bove said not flinching or lowering his eyes.

"Well, be sure you don't," Tom gave a phony smile. "I see you're getting familiar with the ship's medical center. You're learning its functions?" He didn't wait for an answer, instead, he looked at the console, "Pain relief, huh?"

"I have a headache," Bove said.

"Don't we all. I recommend common aspirin; it works for me." He stepped back not moving his eyes from Bove's.

Bove turned and selected a pain medication then looked back at Tom, "This should do it." He stepped around Tom and left.

"Uh," Tom started then looked down, shuffling his feet in indecision.

     *   *   *

Tense from his encounter with Tom, Bove needed a break, something to relax. In his cabin, he found no relief only blank walls staring silently at him. He headed to the kitchen, maybe something to drink would help. The comment, *a restriction of anyone entering the cargo bay,* pushed at him, did Tom know he was there, or only suspected? He tried to ignore it, after all, he was only to fly the ship. It was none of his concern what the cargo was or to whom it was being delivered. Lucus was probably right, Stella would be on her way once she told them what they wanted. She would be fine.

"Hi," Lucy said, cutting into his thoughts as she entered the kitchen.

He looked up at her.

She smiled. "I didn't mean to disturb you," she said.

"No, it's okay. I was just thinking."

"About what?"

"Nothing really, just thinking." He sat across from her, head down, elbows on the table, and ran his hands through his hair.

Lucy looked at him, seriousness tightening her face, then she looked down saying, "So," she took a bite of her sandwich. "What's on your mind?"

"What'd you mean?"

"You're worried, is it about the transit?"

"No," he looked up. *Should I come clean about finding Stella or keep quiet?* He ran a hand through his hair again.

"Well?" Lucy studied him. "Did you go down to

the hold?" And without waiting for an answer, she went on, "What did you find?"

"No," Bove said. "I didn't find anything."

"But you when down there," She poked.

Bove just looked at her, rubbed his head that was starting to ache again, and nodded.

"Well, what's down there?"

"Nothing," Bove said, "Nothing at all."

"Nothing?" Lucy asked

"Well, not nothing, there were crates and boxes, and…"

"And what?" She poked, waited.

"And Stella," Bove whispered.

"Stella? Who's Stella?"

"Quiet." Bove glared at her. "Keep it down. A woman." Bove lowered his voice to whisper. "Don't say a word about this. Tom confronted me about being down there."

"He knows you were there?"

"No, I said I wasn't. They don't want us to know what's going on."

"And what's going on?"

"They're turning her over to the arms dealer, something about information, and they are doing it tomorrow after we transit."

"We can't do anything about that." Lucy stood up taking her plate and glass. She looked down at Bove, "We need to keep our heads down, do what we're told, and get this over with."

"Do nothing?"

"Do nothing."

"You really think so?"

"Yeah. We should stay out of it." Lucy looked down at her empty plate. "I guess."

"Well, I don't know. It doesn't sit well with me."

"Yeah." Lucy shook her head. "Yeah," she whispered.

Twenty-Three

When Lucus called "Enter," Tom stepped into the captain's quarters and stood near the door waiting for Lucus to acknowledge him. He thought about his encounter with Bove in the medical center, *he should be more respectful*. Frown lines creased his forehead and his hand curled into a fist.

"Everything ready?" Lucus cut into Tom's thoughts.

"Huh? Yeah. It's just…"

"What's bothering you?" Lucus cut him off, holding him with his eyes.

"I think Bove was in the hold."

"Why do you say that?"

"I found him in the medical center, and he seemed smug when I asked about being in the hold."

"Smug?"

"Yeah, like he was sure of himself, too sure. And he didn't want to talk."

"He does seem a bit inquisitive. Keep an eye on him. We don't need any interruptions at this point. And make sure he doesn't go to the hold. Understood?" Lucus watched him for a moment, "What did you want?"

"Just that," Tom said, then asked, "What should I do if I find him there?"

"Keep him out and you don't have to worry about that."

*   *   *

At 3:30 Bove settled in his seat on the bridge, looked over at Jack and then at Lucy. "We'll be clear of the Oort Cloud in an hour so let's get to work." He turned back to his console and started entering transit data.

A transit is a process of teleporting a thing—a cup, a table, or a starship--from one place to another. In this case, they would be teleporting a spaceship full of people and cargo from the Sol system to the Tau-Ceti System twelve light-years away. The distance doesn't matter since the process depends on aligning entangled particles in two places and transferring their characteristics from place A to place B. Once the entangled particles align and the characteristics are set, the transit occurs. When this happens the particles in place A disburse and the particles in place B become the same as those in place A. It is like taking an apple, for example, and making all its particles in point B have the same characteristics as particles in point A. The apple is here and an instant later it is there.

Every particle exists as an information matrix that contains descriptors of all its relevant characteristics. Until we understood the frequency of the vibrating strings of fundamental particles, we were unaware of the data matrix and its information. The data matrix includes mass, charge, spin, quantum state, position in space, and moment in time relative to other particles—the data matrix is the particle. The particle passes information about its characteristics to other particles through an exchange of bosons, like a photon.

It is the knowledge of the particle's position in

space and time that allows the use of entanglement for space travel. Before the discovery of the data matrix, the Uncertainty Principle inhibited the use of entanglement for space travel since there was no way of knowing the position of an entangled particle at any given time, and therefore no way to transfer characteristics.

In newer starships, the transit setting is completely automated, and in military ships, it has been fully automated for years because a military ship must be able to transit in an instant. But the Ibex is not a new ship or military, and it takes a while to get the transit controls set.

Bove was responsible for verifying everything was set for a transit and executing it. Once it was complete, he had to verify everything was back online and functioning correctly. Jack would set the destination parameters, so they end up in the correct place, and Lucy had to control the computers that ran all the ship's systems. Dan was responsible for stopping and restarting the engines. This setup would take an hour to complete, which the crew did successfully, and by 4:30 they were ready to execute.

Lucus watched as Bove, Jack, Dan, and Lucy each completed their tasks and ran their final checks to verify everything was correct.

"Engine functions set and ready?" Bove asked.

"All set to go," Dan stated.

"Ship functions set and ready," Lucy said,

"Target destination set and aligned," Jack said.

"On your command," Bove said looking back at Lucus.

"Okay, you're sure?" Lucus asked and when Bove nodded he said, "Then execute."

The sensation during the transit is unlike any other experience. There is an instance of severe pain throughout the body when your particles disburse and reform. It lasts less than a hundredth of a second, but long enough to feel it. Then there is a moment, maybe a few hundredths of a second of disorientation when one does not know where they are or what they are doing. The whole experience is disconcerting but over so quickly it is hardly noticed.

After that instance of transit, they found themselves sitting at the outer edge of the Tau-Ceti System. Shaking his head, Jack looked at the console to verify everything was as it should be, and that they were in the right location. "Target destination established," he said.

"Computers up and running," Lucy said.

"Engines fully operational," Dan said.

"Very good," Lucus glanced at each of them. "Set a course for Ceti-2, to spiral in past Ceti-4."

"That's going to take more than three days." Jack turned to Lucus, "We don't..."

"I'm aware of the time," Lucus interrupted him. "That's the route we're taking."

"Yes Sir." Jack turned back to his console shaking his head.

"If you have something to say, say it," Lucus glared at Jack's back, and Jack simply shook his head again. "Engage at maximum speed," Lucus told Bove.

That must be where they're handing off Stella. Bove thought. *Well, there's nothing I can do about it, I'm sure she'll be all right. All they want is some information and once she tells them what they want, she will be on her way,* Bove rubbed the back of his head where a pain was starting. *The pain of dealing with this old ship*, he thought knowing that was not the cause. He set their velocity to one-third light speed as Lucus had ordered, then leaned back in his chair.

"Very good." Lucus stood up from his chair. "Maintain the course til morning." He left through the side door.

Jack and Dan followed out the main door talking softly as the door slid closed behind them.

Lucy stepped over to Bove. "I told Jack about Stella," she said.

"You did what? I said not to tell anyone." A tightness gripped Bove's chest, he felt like yelling but calmed himself. "What did he say?"

"To stay out of it." Lucy rubbed her hands together. "Like I said."

"What all did you tell him?"

"Just that the package is a woman."

"You think he'll talk to Lucus?"

"I told him not to tell anyone, so, no he won't tell Lucus or Dan."

"Like you didn't."

"Jack's different. I trust him. I just wanted his opinion, what he thought about it."

"I hope you're right. We'll find ourselves out an airlock if we cross Lucus. It seems this delivery is the top priority for him."

"It's a lot of credits. For all of us." Lucy shuffled her feet and looked away from Bove.

"I need to talk to him, make sure he doesn't tell anyone about this. Can you tell him?"

"Yeah, sure." Lucy left.

Bove took a deep breath and stood up, *this is getting out of hand*, he thought.

*   *   *

Bove had just settled in his cabin when a soft knock sounded on his door. He opened it to see lucy and Jack standing in the corridor.

"You wanted to talk to us," Lucy stated not moving from the corridor.

"Come in," Bove stepped aside making room for them to enter.

They entered and stood next to the small desk watching Bove. "So," Lucy glanced at Jack.

"Sit," Bove indicated the chair and bed, Lucy took the chair while Jack sat on the edge of the bed. Bove looked at Jack, "What did Lucy tell you?"

"That there's a woman in the hold." Jack looked up at Bove, "Is that what you wanted to hear?"

Bove sat on the end of the bed facing Jack. "That's all she said?" He asked.

"What's with the questions? She just told me Lucus is delivering the woman to someone." Jack glanced at Lucy and then back to Bove.

"I'm concerned," Bove said. "That we're into something illegal. Something that may cost us, and not just credits." He was worried that this weapons dealer was going to hurt Stella, or worst kill her. But he didn't want to say that to Jack or Lucy, they might not understand.

"It's Lucus' problem. As long as we know nothing about it, we'll be fine." Jack shifted on the bed and took a breath. "There's not much that's illegal out here anyway."

"What'd you think," Bove asked Lucy.

Lucy looked up at Bove, then to Jack. "Uh," she looked down and rubbed her face, took a breath then said, "I agree with Jack. It's Lucus' problem, let him worry about the legality of it." She looked down at her feet avoiding Bove's eyes.

"Do you think Lucus knows what I found out?" Bove asked.

"I didn't tell him," Lucy said softly and glanced at Jack.

"Neither did I. And we won't, right, Lucy?"

"Yeah."

"Tom thinks I was down there. Has he said anything?"

"He doesn't talk to us, so we don't know what he knows." Jack stood up, "If that's all you're concerned about you shouldn't worry. And you should stay out of it. Let Lucus handle things." He turned to Lucy, "Let's go."

Lucy stood up, "Jack's right, stay out of it." She shrugged a shoulder, then headed for the door. Jack followed.

"Yeah," Bove said as he watched them leave.

Twenty-Four

Zabidiah Rice stood six feet five inches tall and weighed over 250 pounds, all muscle. His face matched the brute force his body displayed, it was broad with large cheekbones, a round protruding nose above a dark mustache, and full lips that covered a couple of chipped incisors. A deep brown straggly beard covered a sharp chin, and his small ears were hidden under his long thick brown hair. His eyes were small dark coals making the pupils hard to distinguish. They bore into you like dark lasers burning to the depths of your soul.

Zabi was the product of a broken family. When he was a pre-teen, his drunken father had taken his mother—whom he adored—away and he never saw her again. He never found out what happened to her, only that she had been taken from him. Shortly after his father had returned, refusing to answer any questions about Zabi's mother, he had been killed in illegal dealings; the circumstances which Zabi never discovered. A pre-teen boy was without a family and was soon placed in foster homes.

Zabidiah rebelled running from home after home until he was eighteen. Through all that time he became involved with unsavory groups, finally settling on a career dealing arms to rebel groups from one end of the galaxy to the other. This was just his latest deal, another in a string going back to his younger years.

Unlike his other deals, this one had gone wrong due to Stella taking what was his. And no one took what belonged to Zabidiah.

He sat at the head of the table in his private room off the main bridge of his ship, the Dark Star. His crew of seven filled the other chairs surrounding the table. "So," he said. "Our package is finally arriving. I have received a message from Lucus that he has the goods and is in the system. Tomorrow we will meet him just beyond Ceti-4 outside the asteroid belt and pick up the goods."

The crew, mumbling among themselves, nodded their agreement and waited for more.

He continued. "Here's the plan. We meet Lucus tomorrow probably around noon, so have an early lunch. Ha. Ha." He showed his chipped teeth, then stopped. The crew chuckled along with him and stopped with him. "They will come in their shuttle and meet ours. Once we dock shuttle to shuttle, they will bring the package to us and we will have the credits for them, except we are not going to give them the credits. If there's any issue with that, we will deal with it. Understood?"

"What do we do if they give us trouble?" Samuel asked.

"Sam," Zabi said. "You are always the one to ask. If they have weapons, we will have to shoot them."

Ruby spoke up. "That will turn into a tough situation."

"Not really," Luke added. "If they have weapons, they won't be as good as ours, and we have them outnumbered. They would be fools to try to fight us."

"Right," Zabi added. "They might hurt one or two of us, but we will annihilate them."

"I'd pay them a token amount to keep them off our backs," Mila said.

"A woman's compassion." Zabi glared at her. "They're late and don't deserve a single credit, and if they come after us, we will annihilate them."

"Do you want all of us there?" Alejandro asked.

"Four of us will meet them, you, Luke, and Ruby. And me, of course. The rest of you will have our backs from the ship. If anything goes wrong, we can take them out. They, or at least Lucus, knows what firepower we have on this ship and would be foolish to try anything."

"So that's the plan?" Samuel asked, looking at each crew member.

"Yes," Zabi smiled. "That's the plan. And once we have the girl back here safely, we will find out where she hid our weapons." He turned his eyes on each member of his crew studying their faces for any concern, and misgivings.

"What if she doesn't give us the weapons?" Sam asked.

"Oh, she'll give us the weapons," Zabi smiled, a gleam in his eye. "She'll live long enough to tell us where they are, then she can die."

Once I have her, Zabi thought. *I will extract the information however I have to. If she refuses, I can always take her fingernails, one by one. Or her fingers. Removing pieces of someone's body is always an effective way to get information. People hate to watch themselves being cut up. Not to think about the pain it causes. And of course, you always promise to let them live no matter how much you take from them. The more they think about life with no fingers, hands, or arms, the more likely they are to talk and stop the process. But it makes no difference, they all die in the end. I just can't let them go walking around telling everyone what I've done. The final act is always so satisfying, letting them think it's over and they're safe, then telling them they are to die anyway. The look on their faces is priceless, disbelief and shock. Then the pleading starts, the bargaining, the unfairness of it, but it's to no avail. They must go in the end.*

The crew shifted in their seats, not from fear or revulsion, but desire. There were lots of credits tied up with the weapons they had lost and getting them back meant their pay would be coming soon. None of them cared about Stella or her fate, they cared about their pay and what they could do with it. They were an unsavory bunch, gamblers and carousers looking for the next thrill, the next big score. And Stella was holding an opportunity in her hands which Zabi intended to pry loose.

But then there are those like Stella, Zabi thought. *That can be useful to the crew. She is a looker and very appealing. The crew could have lots of fun with her before I dispose of her, and they will be so grateful for the pleasure—except maybe Ruby and Mila. I'll have to find something else for them. A good beating might open Stella's mouth and that will leave her intact for the crew's enjoyment. Then maybe send her out the airlock, or just vent the air and watch her suffocate. After all, she did take my weapons, and for that, she does not deserve to live.*

"Captain," Carter broke into his thoughts. "Will we transit once we have her?"

"Huh," Zabi shook his head to clear his

thoughts. "Uh, no. We have to find the weapons first. They may be right here in the system, so first we get the information from the girl, get the weapons and deliver them, then we transit."

"Okay," Carter leaned back in his chair.

"Now we need to check the ship, make sure everything is operational including the transit module. Make sure the weapons are ready. This whole delivery should be over in twenty minutes. So, let's get to it and be prepared for tomorrow."

The crew disbursed and headed out to complete their tasks of checking the ship. The Dark Star was a warship fully armed with forward and rear guns, as well as side guns. All weapons were located to sight the top and bottom of the ship and in all directions around it. There were heavy weapons able to take out the largest ships currently made with ranges of up to three to four thousand meters. All the missiles in their arsenal were accurate up to twenty-five thousand meters and self-guided once the target schematics were entered. It was a formable ship and well able to defend itself.

Zabi was not worried about Lucus' ship, but he planned to disable it to be on the safe side. *It will keep them off our back while we retrieve our weapons*, he thought.

Twenty-Five

The Ibex's course was set to spiral around Tau-Ceti to Ceti-4. The rendezvous with the weapons dealer was to take place inside the orbit of Ceti-4. *How,* Bove wondered, *could Lucus hand Stella over for credits? With no concern for her?* In all his First Encounter missions he never considered the credits, his only concern was finding and preserving unique species that lived throughout the galaxy. *By tomorrow it would all be over*, he thought. Then he would see where he stood with this ship and crew.

His time with the First Encounter Team was finished, no more missions, no more visions. He was done and would never go back, and if this didn't work out, he would find something else. There are plenty of ships that need piloting and there will be one that can use someone like him. So, if this is a one-time deal there will be others. Still, turning over a woman for profit was wrong—but what could he do?

It was late evening by the time he had eaten dinner and was back in his cabin ready to sleep. It had been an eventful couple of days and was due to become even more so. He settled in his bunk, but sleep eluded him, his mind kept running through the events of the last couple of days, being hired to pilot the ship, finding Stella, the transfer being earlier than Lucus had told him, and in a different place. He wondered about this arms dealer, Zabi, Stella had called him. From what he knew about arms dealers, and it wasn't much, they were not forgiving, so whatever the reason was for getting Stella it couldn't be good. In fact, it may be bad for any of the crew.

As he thought about tomorrow all manner of scenarios came to mind—Zabi taking Stella and stranding the rest of them in the middle of the Ceti system, taking the crew along with Stella for sale to the highest bidder, taking Stella and shooting the crew, and…

Sleep captured him displacing the thoughts of dire outcomes with dreams. He was sitting in a small room with two arched doorways, one to his left where he could see a high hill with a path curving up to the top. Through the arch to his right was a vast prairie of short grass surrounded in the distance by mountains on the horizon with gray wisps of clouds in the sky above. Nestled in the prairie was a bog filled with putrid water that gave off the smell of rot and death.

Bove coughed the stench from his nose and lungs then looked away. In the center of the room was a fountain bubbling water into a basin and on the walls were murals of trees and animals of every variety. The ceiling was a sky covered with clouds and birds.

Across the room sat a gray-haired man in a robe rippling in shades of red. He watched Bove with blue eyes hard as shining crystals. His mouth was a firm straight line and his nose flared with each breath.

"Who are you?" Bove ask forgetting the smell of the bog.

"You know who I am." Tanka waved a hand toward the doorway facing the prairie and the air became fresh. "And you know why I'm here. You have made commitments."

"Commitments?" Bove asked, wishing he could wake. He knew of this from his visions on Kryth and on the Starship Mars. He knew that was why Tanka was with him, but he didn't want anything to do with him or the visions.

"I thought I was through with the visions. You told me I would be free once I returned to the ship."

"Oh, you are free. You can do as you wish, but you did commit to do the right thing no matter what it was. Do you remember?" Tanka watched as Bove realized he was faced with just the situation he had committed to stop.

He felt a chill run through his body as the truth struck him. He had committed to helping anyone being mistreated no matter who or how the mistreatment was conducted. He had committed to help when someone's well-being was threatened no matter how serious or trivial the threat was. And Stella was about to be turned over to someone that could do great harm to her. But...

"I can do nothing about this situation," he said.

"That is your choice." Tanka looked into Bove's eyes. "You can honor your commitments, or you can return to the bog. You remember the bog with its penetrating stench and deadly waters?"

"This isn't real, it's a dream and I can wake from it."

"No, Bove, it is a vision. And as I have explained before you are both here and there and only the termination of the vision can return you to the *there*. If you fail to follow your commitment you will be returned to the bog and the bog is where you will stay."

"For being free of your visions you leave me

little choice."

"You can choose to honor your commitments, or not. Those are your choices."

"You mean death because that's what I'll get if I try to help Stella or the bog that has the same result. What choice is that?"

"And that is as it should be," Tanka said.

"What do you mean by that. I should be able to do as I please."

"You can."

"Without having to die. Two choices with the same outcome is no choice."

"That is as it is." Tanka stared at Bove waiting.

Bove stood up and looked around the small room. The doorways were no longer there, they had become walls blending into the murals. *Great*, He thought. There was only one thing he could do, and he knew it. If he chose to not help Stella, he would return to the bog where he would die. He knew that for certain. The waters of the bog were deadly to the touch and there was no way out. A slow death of starvation. He turned to Tanka and ran a hand through his hair. Anger flared and his hands turned into fists, he held his breath and closed his eyes.

When he opened them, Tanka's blue eyes still burned into him seeking an answer.

"Okay! I'll try to help Stella." Bove lowered his head with a slight shake. "Now terminate the vision," he said quietly.

"As you wish," Tanka waved his right hand from his left shoulder across his face.

Bove woke with a jerk, "What the hell..." He sat up and looked around to verify he was still on the ship, in his cabin. Nothing had changed. He checked the time, ten forty, only fifteen minutes since he lay down to sleep. *What just happened*, he thought. *I was back on the three hills looking at the bog. The bog where I woke, where I could have died! The hills where I committed to helping someone in danger.* "Oh shit!"

He felt back on his bunk realizing his commitment. He must help or return to the bog where he would remain. His choices were to do nothing and die, or die trying to save Stella.

He had to stop the transfer, but how? Turning in his bunk he tried to create a plan. *Tomorrow the transfer will happen, so what can I do? Will Lucy or Jack help? If they know what's going down, I think they will. But first I need a plan.* He turned in his bunk thinking about the transfer, how it will happen, where it will happen. He had no idea how to stop it. *Shit,* he thought, then considered, *they're meeting in open space, docking shuttle to shuttle. Then they will move Stella to Zabi's shuttle--that's what I would do. So how am I going to stop this?* As he pondered his options sleep soon eased him into a dreamless void of darkness.

His alarm chimed pulling him from sleep into a stupor of wakefulness. "Oooh!" he said shaking his head to wake up. He sat up in his bunk silenced the alarm, stretched his arms and legs, and yawned, *I have a plan*, he thought.

Twenty-Six

Bove's plan was simple if Lucy and Jack would help. If not, Lucus would turn Stella over to Zabi and that would be the end of it. And most likely the end of Bove.

He stopped by the kitchen hoping to find Lucy or Jack but to his disappointment, no one was there. After breakfast, he headed to the bridge where the crew was at their consoles hard at work.

"Where have you been?" Jack looked up as Bove slid into his seat.

"I overslept," Bove glanced at Jack, then in a low voice so Dan couldn't hear he said, "I need to talk to you and Lucy." He hoped they would help save Stella. Lucy had seemed concerned, but would she help when the time came. Wondering if either would help him was pressing on his mind when Lucus entered the bridge and took his seat.

"Status?" Lucus asked.

"On course." Bove felt Lucus' eyes on his back. "We will be to Ceti-2 in two days." *But*, Bove thought, *that's not where we're going, is it Lucus?* There was little time to get Jack and Lucy away to ask for their help. He knew the hand-off would be today, but when, was one question, and how to get with Jack and Lucy was another. And the third, how to implement his plan.

"Anyone hungry?" he asked looking at Jack with a nod then turning to Lucy and tipping his head toward the door. She looked back with a furrowed brow and a tipped head. Bove nodded and stood heading out.

Jack got up saying, "I did miss breakfast, you cooking?"

"Yeah," Bove said. "You coming?" He asked Lucy, ignoring Dan and Lucus.

"I could use some food too," Lucus said standing up. "How about you, Dan?" He asked, then asked Bove, "What do you cook?"

"Regular stuff," Bove answered trying to come up with a way to exclude him and Dan with no success.

"I'm good," Lucy said, "I'll get something at lunch."

Great, Bove thought, *Lucus wants to come, and Lucy wants to stay. What crap!*

Beeee! Beeee! The alarm blasted. Everyone stopped and turned to Lucy.

"System malfunction." Lucy's voice was stressed. She cleared her throat. "There's a glitch in the primary navigation alignment function. It's going to take time to correct it. Lucus, I need command control to correct this."

Lucus sat back down, "Jack what's your assessment?"

Jack bend over at his console then turned to Lucy who looked back with a serious expression. He turned back to Lucus, "She's right. This is serious."

"Very well," Lucus said punching a couple of buttons on his console, "You have control. How long is this going to take?"

"No more than an hour. I'll need to work from the computer's main terminal." Lucy tapped keys on her console, glancing up at the main viewing screen from time to time.

"Get on with it," Lucus said. "I'll be in my office if you need me." He got up and left by the side door.

"What's going on?" Dan turned in his chair to face the others. "Is that going to affect our route?"

"If Lucy can't fix it, we'll have to manually control ship."

"So?"

"Well, we could be off-target by a few hundred kilometers. Enough to miss our meeting for the delivery of the package."

"Oh…" Dan turned back facing his console, then turned back, "She can fix it, right?"

"Yeah, in a couple of hours."

"Did you want to get something to eat?" Bove asked Dan

"I'll stay here to make sure everything goes well."

Lucy smiled at him then turned to Bove. "I'll be in the computer control room. Please don't disturb me, this is going to take some concentration and I'll need peace and quiet." She stood and walked out through the main bridge door."

Jack followed Bove out after Lucy who stopped in front of the computer main server room--halfway down the main corridor from the bridge.

"What's up?" Jack studied Lucy as she opened the door to the computer room and slipped through holding the door for Bove and Jack. "There wasn't a glitch in anything." He let the door slide shut and stood there waiting for an answer.

"Where's Tom?" Bove asked.

"Who knows," Lucy said.

"Probably in the observation room, or the hold. That's where he spends most of his time." Jack glanced at Lucy then back to Bove, "Tell me what's up?"

"Yeah, Bove, what's up?" Lucy asked.

"This delivery..." Bove was interrupted.

"No," Lucy interjected, "I told you to leave it! Do nothing!"

"But you didn't mean it. Did you?" Bove stared at Lucy until she lowered her head looking at her feet. "Listen, it's not as simple as that."

"Yeah, why not?" Jack asked.

"Because..." Bove stopped unsure how to proceed. He ran a hand through his hair and leaned against the counter.

"Because," Lucy cut in. "You've got a soft spot, or some kind of hero complex, that's why."

"Wait," Bove crossed his arms over his chest and then looked at both Jack and Lucy. "I have to do this. I don't have a choice. And if you won't help, I'll do it alone."

"What are you talking about?" Jack asked.

"Stopping Lucus from turning Stella over," Bove said. "It can't happen."

"What do you mean, of course, it will happen. We can't stop it." Jack glared at Bove. "Tom won't let anyone interfere. He's Lucus' right-hand man and he makes sure things go the way Lucus wants. You don't want to mess with him." Jack reached to the door to leave.

"We can stop it," Bove stated and waited to see if Jack would listen or leave.

Jack hesitated, holding his hand near the door panel. He turned back to Bove taking a breath. "Does that mean you're going to try?"

"What?" Lucy's eyes widened and she dropped into the chair in front of the console.

"That's ludicrous!" Jack looked at Bove then Lucy for support.

"It's a woman's life," Bove said.

Lucy couldn't help but think Bove was right. Yet fear clutched her gut with a vice grip. She rubbed her face with open palms.

"That's suicide." Jack clenched his fists like he was ready to punch Bove but opened his hands instead. "Lucus has the only gun on the ship and he's not averse to using it. Just give him a reason and you'll find yourself out the airlock. No, you can't stop it." Jack took a couple of steps around the small room shaking his head, contemplating the situation.

"Listen," Bove said, "I have a plan that should work, but I'll need your help."

"Again, no." Jack glared at him.

"Hear him out," Lucy looked up at Jack. She gripped the arms of the chair, "we're talking about a woman's life."

"A woman's life?" He turned to Bove. "What do you mean *a woman's life?*"

"Yeah." Bove said, "Lucus is going to turn her over to the arms dealer who will probably kill her. That's why we have to try to stop this."

"Kill her?" Jack shook his head.

"Jack, you know as well as I do what's going to happen," Bove said. "Once she's turned over, she's as good as dead." He glared at Jack until Jack stopped looking back at him. "Here's what I propose," he said.

Jack opened his mouth, then closed it again, shook his head, and took a deep breath, "Okay," he said.

Lucy nodded her head, "go on."

"The transfer will be either shuttle to shuttle, or in the dealer's ship. They won't come here. Either way, we have to keep Lucus from getting Stella in the shuttle."

"Stella?" Jack said questions flashing across his face, "Seems you're pretty familiar with her, what's been going on?"

"Jack," Lucy said, "Leave it be." She turned to Bove, "Go on."

"If Lucus gets her to the shuttle there will be no chance of getting her back. I figure it'll be an easy task to grab her before Lucus does. Then we take the ship and get out of town."

"Take the ship?" Lucy shook her head and looked down at her hands folded in her lap.

"I see several problems in your plan," Jack said. "First, like I said, Lucus has the only gun on the ship and I'm sure he won't hesitate to shoot anyone that tries to interfere. Second the arms dealer we're delivering to, will have a heavily armed ship well able to take us out, that's the way arms dealers are. Third, if we take his package, he will be after us until the end of time. Other than that, it's a good plan.

Lucy nodded still looking at her hands in her lap, "Jack's right."

"Well," Bove said. "We need to tip the odds. Are there no other weapons on board?"

"There's an armory at the end of the corridor, but it's locked we don't have the code." Jack looked at Lucy and back to Bove. "There's only a couple of phasers and a couple of blaster rifles. That's it if Tom hasn't taken them. Even if he hasn't, how do we get into it?"

"One thing at a time," Bove said, "You said the arms dealer will have a heavily armed ship, what weapons are on this ship?"

"Weapons?" Jack asked, "We don't have any weapons, it's a cargo ship, no need for weapons."

"Nothing?" Bove asked.

"There are a couple of small blasters for blowing space rock out of the way, but they are not very powerful," Jack looked doubtful.

"Okay, "Bove rubbed his brow. "If they think Stella is gone, dead, they won't be after us. So, we have to make it look like she gets killed before the delivery takes place."

"What's to stop them from blowing the ship to bits if they think their package is dead?" Jack asked. "And what about the weapons, the armory?"

"And the fact that they have weapons on their ship that we don't?" Lucy added.

"One thing at a time," Bove said. "We need to think this through from step one to the end." He turned away and rubbed his forehead, then ran his fingers through his hair. *What the hell am I going to do?* he thought. *How am I going to stop this? Are Lucy and Jack in it with me? Who knows? They seem to be interested. But when it comes to confronting Lucus will they be there? Or will they turn on me? Can I trust them?*

He looked at Lucy then Jack noting their confused faces, "Are you with me?" he asked.

"Well," Jack started but Lucy interrupted.

"We don't know," she said. "Right Jack?"

Jack nodded. "This is all well and good, but Lucus and Tom are not going to let this go. And the arms dealer will be after us forever. I think this is a lot of bull. Let Lucus do what he needs to do and let's go on to greener pastures."

"Fine," Bove said. "Do what you think is right, let Lucus turn Stella over to the asshole that will probably kill her, but that's okay. I hope you can live with that while you're spending your credits on whatever you think is more important than human life."

Lucy and Jack looked at Bove like he was crazy. "What are you saying?" Jack asked.

"I am going to do something one way or another. That's what I'm saying!" Bove slammed his hand on the counter. "If you are not going to help me, at least you can not stop me?"

"If you really need us, we'll back you up," Lucy said.

Jack looked at the ceiling and shook his head. "Yeah, okay." He glanced at Lucy. "But I don't like it."

"Well," Bove said. "I really need you. So, here's what we'll do. I'll sneak into the cargo bay and get Stella, then stash her someplace safe. We'll tell Lucus to tell the arms dealers there's a delay. Then we will transit to another system."

"Transit?" Jack glared at Bove. "It'll take an hour to prep and what, a half a day to get to a transit point?"

"That won't work," Lucy added.

"Don't worry about a transit point. You can transit out from any place. It's entering a system from a transit that's dangerous. So, we need to get ready beforehand. Jack, you, and Lucy should go to the bridge and get ready to transit, send us anywhere away from here. I'll get Stella to a safe place. Then we can talk to Lucus.

"Yeah, right. How are you going to do that?" Jack asked glancing at Lucy.

"I'll get a weapon from the armory and then Lucus and Tom will have to listen to us."

"Good luck with that," Jack said. "I'll see if we can get everything set for a transit. If everything goes south, we can at least get out of here. Good luck," he said and stood to leave. "You coming?" He asked Lucy.

She shook her head, "I'm supposed to be fixing a problem, remember?"

"Can you two handle everything for a transit?" Bove asked.

Jack stopped, "Yeah," he said and left.

I'm going to have to trust him, Bove thought as the door slid shut. *If they tell Lucus what I'm up to, everything will be lost. I'll find myself out the airlock or turned over to Zabi along with Stella.*

"I'll see you on the bridge," he told Lucy and followed Jack out the door.

*   *   *

Bove headed for the kitchen where he found flour and a soft cloth, he stashed them in his pocket and headed to the armory wondering where Tom was. He wasn't concerned about Dan, he seemed to want to stay out of things, and he might still be on the bridge. Lucus was in this office and hopefully Tom was with him, or in the cargo bay. Although that would be a problem getting Stella.

The armory had a coded lock securing it. Bove studied it for a couple of minutes then took the flour and cloth from his pocket. He blew the flour on the lock then lightly brushed any excess away. The flour covered the ten keys and was sticking to the four most used. Now all he had to do was figure out the sequence of the keys to open the lock.

He studied the lock more closely trying to note differences in the amount of powder on each key. He noticed three of the keys held more powder than the others indicating they were used first. With six combinations for the three keys, Bove quickly tried each one pressing the last key after each try. On the third try, it opened.

He wiped the flour from the keys and entered the armory to discover a single laser pistol and a blaster rifle. He took both, locked the armory, and holding his breath he hurried down the corridor to the lift hoping no one came into the corridor before he could get into the lift going down. Sweat beaded on his forehead as he waited for the lift door to open, and when it did, he stepped in and pushed the button for deck four. He wiped his forehead and took a deep breath calming his nerves. Once in his cabin, he stashed the weapons in a cabinet just as an announcement came over the intercom.

"Crew to the bridge, Crew to the bridge."

What now? he thought as he headed out. Entering the bridge he asked, "What's up?"

"Rendezvous," Lucus said. "We've arrived at our contact."

"In space," Bove asked.

"Yeah, in space. You have a problem with that?" Lucus stared at Bove.

"Are we docking and to what?" He shot back at Lucus as he sat at his console.

"No, we're not docking. Tom and I'll be taking the shuttle to meet our client. You should see a ship shortly, just approach it to about a thousand meters and stay with it. Can you do that?"

"No problem," Bove said. He looked at Jack then over at Lucy. Both were busy working at their consoles.

"Let me know when you've established a matching vector. I'll be in the shuttle with Tom." Lucus got up. Stopped at the door as it slid open, "Do you have the ship yet?"

Bove turned and looked at Lucus, "Yeah, it's on the screen." He paused for a moment then added, "a shuttle-to-shuttle dock can be tricky, maybe I should pilot the shuttle. I've done that many times."

"No need," Lucus said. "Tom can handle it." And he left letting the door slide shut behind him.

"Shit!" Bove said.

"What?" Jack asked.

Dan turned from his console, "What's going on? All this secrecy."

"Tell him," Lucy said.

"Are you ready to transit?" Bove asked.

"Almost," Lucy answered and glanced at Bove. "It was hard to work it with Lucus watching, but we're almost there. Now tell Dan."

Bove nodded and turned to Dan, "Lucus has a woman that he's turning over to Zabi—the arms dealer—and I have to stop it. So, that said, I have to get to the shuttle and get her out of there. They're going to launch the shuttle when we match up with the other ship." Bove turned back to his console and checked the location of the other ship. They were four thousand meters and closing fast. He cut the speed and checked the ETA—four minutes twenty seconds. "How long until we can transit?"

"Three minutes," Lucy said.

"They've locked weapons on us," Jack said.

"Oh great!" Bove felt a shiver run up his spine. He paused for an instant and took a deep breath.

"If we try to transit, they'll fire, we won't make it," Lucy said.

"What are you doing?" Dan demanded. "You're going to get us killed if you try to transit. We're in the middle of a star system!"

"Can you sabotage the shuttle?" Bove ignored Dan's outburst.

"How?" Lucy asked.

"I don't care., do anything. What about you, Dan, can you do something?"

"I'm not getting involved," Dan answered. "Lucus has the only laser and he's not averse to using it. I'd rather be on his good side."

"I have a laser too, and a rifle," Bove stated matter-of-factly.

"I'll see if I can do something," Lucy said.

"Are you guys helping with this?" Dan looked at both Jack and Lucy.

"Yeah, a bit," Jack said.

"Good," Bove said to Lucy. He got up and headed for the door., "I'll be back." He stopped, turned back, "Can we do any damage with the blaster in the front of the ship?" He asked,

"Well, yeah," Jack said, "but they are armed to the teeth. They'll take us out if we fire on them."

"Can you locate their weapon's control, or targeting computer and damage that?"

"I can try," Lucy said, "But I can't do both."

"Stop the shuttle first," Bove stated as he headed out the door.

"Are you guys crazy?" Dan gripped the arms of his chair. "You know if Lucus thinks you have anything

193

to do with stopping him, you'll be out the airlock. You make sure he knows I have nothing to do with this." He spun around putting his back to Jack and Lucy.

Jack turned to him. "You make sure you stay quiet about us. Ya got that?"

"Whatever," Dan said to his console.

*   *   *

Lucus entered the shuttle and sat in the right seat next to Tom, "You have our package?" he asked.

"Safe and secure in the hold," Tom answered.

"Very good. Once Bove stops us we'll contact Zabi for the meet. It should go smooth." Lucus smiled and leaned back in his seat. "Everything ready to launch?"

"Yep," Tom said, "the shuttle is clear to fly, all functions are operating normally. All we have to do is open the door and leave. Just let me know when you're ready."

"Should be in a minute or two. You got their ship on the monitor?"

"Yeah."

"Good. Bove will stop us at a thousand meters, then it's a go."

Twenty-Seven

Bove sat on his bunk with the blaster and pistol lying across his lap. *What am I going to do?* He wondered, *the rifle was for Jack, but will he use it? Lucy won't. Does it matter?* He ran a hand through his hair and took a deep breath. *How am I going to get Stella? I have to get on the shuttle with Lucus and Tom and they're probably ready to launch. There's no time to get there and save her.* He dropped his head into his hands shaking it in despair.

Suddenly he was no longer sitting on his bunk. He was sitting on grass with tall reeds rising above him, the noxious smell of rotting vegetation burned his nostrils, and the memory of the bog flooded back to him. The rot of death from the water filled the air and, his nose and throat. Before him lay the path to the WayGate. He leaped to his feet and ran following the path through the bog to the WayGate and the way out, but when he arrived there was no doorway. He fell against it hands pressed on the solid surface where a doorway should be. He hung his head taking deep breaths while pressing the wall as if to push through.

"You made the right choice. Now you must act," Tanka said.

Bove spun around to see Tanka standing before him in a rode of green, shifting like a forest in the breeze. His eyes bore into Bove; blue lasers burning into his soul.

"You are giving up when there're still opportunities to pursue. You committed to do whatever it takes to resolve the situation and you have stopped before every path has been considered." Tanka looked at Bove assisting his resolve.

"What more can I do?" Bove glanced at Tanka, then shifted his eyes to the first hill raising into the clear sky.

What more? Tanka glared at him and threw his arms up, "You can save the girl! You fool! That's what you committed to. If you quit, you will remain in the bog." With that Tanka vanished leaving Bove standing at the WayGate with nowhere to go but back into the bog.

"Shit!" Bove yelled and slammed his hand against the WayGate wall. "I'll save Stella!" Suddenly he was sitting on his bunk again disorientated and confused, but only for a moment. The realization struck, shaking him from head to foot. *Okay, I can do this.* He stood determination flooding into him. He shook his body loosening his muscles and driving the tension and anxiety from his mind. He focused, remembering the clarity needed for a First Encounter mission. Control returned. He put the rifle over his shoulder, the pistol in his waistband, and started for the shuttle to get Stella.

*   *   *

The entrance to the shuttle bay was across the holding area from where Bove stood. *I don't need the rifle,* he thought leaning it against the wall. Taking a breath to steady himself, he thought, *okay this is it; this is what I have committed to.* He entered the code to open the shuttle bay airlock and stepped in leaving it open so the shuttle couldn't launch. The shuttle sitting in front of him had its door open and was clearly inactive. The second shuttle on the far side of the bay was where Stella, Tom, and Lucus were.

Less than three minutes before Jack stops the ship for the exchange, he considered. *And they can override the open airlock from inside the shuttle to launch. They do that and I'll be out the bay door with them.*

*   *   *

Tom turned to Lucus. "Bove's out there. What's he doing?"

"How should I know," Lucus tapped the arm of his seat with his fingers. "Get on the intercom and tell him to get out of the bay. Tell him we're going to launch whether he's there or not."

"Okay," Tom flipped the intercom switch. "What do you think he's doing?"

"He wants to save Stella," Lucus said matter-of-factly. "I thought he would try this. Maybe we should launch and not worry about him."

"It's your call." Tom shifted in his seat and ran his hand along his collar. "Should I close the airlock and warn him?"

"Yeah, close the airlock and prepare to launch."

Tom looked at Lucus for a moment. "Should I warn him?" He pushed his shoulders back and spread his fingers out over the console – away from the controls.

"Close the shuttle bay airlock."

Tom flipped the switch to override the open airlock and waited. The green light glowed showing the airlock was secure, at the same time an alarm sounded, and a red light flashed on indicating the shuttle door had been breached.

"What the hell!" Lucus exclaimed. "What's that?"

"Bove opened the shuttle door."

"Get out there and stop him. Shoot him if you have to!" Lucus slammed his hand against the console, "Shit!"

*   *   *

Bove heard the airlock close. *No time,* he thought, *Gota do something*.

He rushed around the shuttle and keyed in the code to open the shuttle door, thanking himself for reading the operations manual while they had waited to reach the transit point in the Sol system. The door slid open and he stepped in.

An alarm announced the breach of the shuttle door and stated that the launch was delayed until the breach was corrected. *Great*, Bove thought, *they know I'm in here*. He pulled the laser pistol from his belt and checked the area.

The shuttle is a small ship, the entry had an airlock with two doors—one to the outside and the other going into the shuttle. Both doors could be left open for easy access while in the shuttle bay. Bove left both open. Inside was a short corridor, to the right was the door to the cockpit and to the left was the cargo bay. Both doors were closed leaving the short entry passage isolated. Bove immediately opened the cargo bay door and looked in. He was greeted by a wrench just missing his head—lucky he only looked and didn't step through the door.

"Stella!" He stepped back holding up a hand, "It's Bove. Get outa there." But before she could move Tom came through the other door from the cockpit pointing a pistol at Bove.

"What are you doing?" he demanded "Get off this shuttle!"

Bove turned, fired from his hip just missing Tom, "Get out!" He yelled at Stella.

Tom fell back through the door, Stella darted past Bove into the shuttle bay, Tom fired a shot at Bove missing over his shoulder and searing the bulkhead behind him. Bove dashed out the door after Stella, firing as he went and forcing Tom back into the cockpit. Once out of the shuttle he punched the code to lock the shuttle door and watched it slide closed.

He ran around the shuttle to the bay door and saw Stella through the open airlock. She was at the door to the corridor holding the blaster to her shoulder pointing at Bove.

"You're not going to shoot me, are you?" Bove stepped through the airlock toward her.

"No." Stella lowered the blaster but kept it pressed to her shoulder. "It's for Tom if he comes through."

"Get out of here and call the lift?"

"Sure." Stella glanced over her shoulder and headed out of the holding area.

*   *   *

Lucy checked the status of the transit settings, "We're good to go," she said to Jack just as the intercom crackled with Lucus' voice, "Attention all hands, Bove has interfered with our delivery and is to be apprehended upon sight."

"A shuttle has been launched from the other ship heading our way," Jack turned to Lucy fear flashed across his face.

"What should we do?" Lucy's face turned pale.

She clasped her hands in her lap unable to move.

"If Bove comes up here we'll grab him," Dan said.

"No! We won't grab him." Jack turned to Dan, "I wonder where he is?" He asked no one in particular, then without waiting for an answer he continued, "I guess we're as much in the dark as Lucus and Tom. I don't know what he's doing, do you?" He looked at Lucy.

Lucy shook her head, "No…"

"Notify the approaching shuttle there is a delay," Lucus instructed over the intercom.

"Well there's your answer," Dan said. "I'll see if I can locate him. And if he comes here, I'm going to grab him. You guys do what you want."

Lucy punched buttons and said, "Hailing approaching shuttle, identify yourself."

"We're here for our package, is there a problem?" The voice was flat, all business and serious as hell.

"Identify yourself," Lucy repeated.

"You don't need an identification; you need to deliver our goods. Now I repeat, is there a problem?"

"There's a slight delay," Lucy glanced at Jack.

"We're coming aboard." A shiver ran up Lucy's back.

"Oh shit!" Jack paled. "Tell Lucus."

Dan dropped into his seat his face turning white. "Don't let them on board."

Lucy flipped the intercom switch to the shuttle, "Lucus," she said, "the shuttle from the other ship said they are coming aboard."

"No," Lucus shouted. "Delay them!"

*   *   *

Tom tried the airlock and finding it locked he returned to the cockpit. He typed in the override code to open it, then rushed back and out into the shuttle bay just as the door slid shut in front of Bove. "Stop!" he yelled rushing into the holding area, pistol raised but holding his fire.

Bove met Stella in front of the lift, she was holding the door for him. They entered and headed for deck three.

"What now?" Stella asked.

"Come with me," Bove said jamming the lift door open on Deck Three--the crew cabins-- Bove opened the cabin across from his, "Get in there and hide," he said, "I'll deal with Tom and Lucus."

"Be safe," Stella smiled at him, stepped into the cabin, and closed the door.

Bove nodded as the door cut him off from her. He headed for the bridge.

        *   *   *

"Dock with their ship," Zabi said, "We're going to get our goods."

"They outnumber us," Luke looked back at Zabi.

"They're weak and afraid, they won't be a problem."

"Approaching the ship," Al said, "We can dock in thirty seconds."

Zabi watched as they approached the ship tapping his fingers on the arm of his chair. The shuttle slowly approached the ship until it was touching the docking port. Al punched several buttons and touched the controls to bring the shuttle steadily to the docking port. A gentle bump ran through it as the clamps on the Ibex closed.

"Docked," Al said.

"Well," Zabi said, "Let's get our goods. Open the docking port."

Ruby stood up and checked her pistol. "You wait here," Zabi said to her.

Al punched a couple of other buttons and the lights on the console turned green. "Port open," he said.

*   *   *

"Docking bay entry open." Blasted through the bridge.

"What?" Jack looked up and turned towards the bridge entrance.

"They boarded," Lucy turned towards Jack. "Where's Bove?"

"I'm here," Bove said coming in. "We've got a problem."

"You're not kidding," Dan said. "The arms dealer just docked. They're on the ship."

"Tom and Lucus are after me," Bove said.

"Maybe we should help them," Dan said standing up to confront Bove.

"Who? Lucus?" Jack asked.

"Are you going to be a problem?" Bove leveled his pistol at Dan.

"No," Dan shook his head and raised his hands, and dropped back into his seat. "No, no problem."

"What are we going to do?" Lucy asked.

"Did you get the package?" Jack asked.

"You mean Stella?" Bove turned to Jack. "I hid her."

"Where," Lucy asked.

"You don't need to know. If worst comes to worst, you'll be better off not knowing anything."

"Okay…" Lucy turned back to her console-like

nothing was out of the ordinary.

Dan looked around then turned back to his console.

"Do you have any more weapons?" Jack asked.

"A blaster but Stella has it."

"Great!" Jack clenched his hands into fists. "How are we supposed to do anything?"

"Just hold on," Bove held up a hand, "Let me think."

They're on the ship. Bove thought, *we have a single pistol, Tom and Lucus are after me...* He dropped his head wondering how he can get out of this situation when the bridge door slid open, and Tom rushed in.

"You!" he said pointing his laser pistol at Bove. "This is your fault."

"We've been boarded," Bove looked at Tom, then Jack. "We need to deal with them."

Tom looked at Jack who nodded. "Zabi will do anything to get his package," Tom said, then turned to Bove. "You shit!" he said. "I should blast you to hell right now."

"I'm the only one who knows where Stella is," Bove said.

"Tom," Jack said, "think about it. They'll torture all of us then rip the ship apart to get her. We've got to stop them. All of us together."

Tom looked at Jack, then Lucy, who nodded, and back to Bove.

Lucus burst through the door, "What the hell, Bove!" he said, "They're on my ship!"

"Calm down," Tom said. "Jack has a point."

"What?" Lucus glared at Tom.

"We, all of us, have to stop them. Get them off

our ship."

"What?" Lucus repeated, looking at his crew one by one.

"Get them off our ship," Tom said. "You can still get a deal once they're gone. We'll still have Stella to give them."

"What?" Lucus glared at Tom then turned to Bove.

"Get them off the ship." Tom raised his voice and glared back at Lucus, "then give them Stella, we can do that."

Lucus looked at Tom slowly nodding, "Yeah, you're right. Let's get them off the ship first."

Just then the bridge door opened and Zabi stepped in followed by Al and Luke. They spread across the bridge covering everyone. "Drop your weapons," Zabi pointed his pistol at Lucus. "You are outnumbered, and my colleagues will not hesitate to fire on you.

"Wait," Lucus held up a hand. "We can work this out. There is no intention of stiffing you, we have the girl and will deliver her."

"Where is she?" Zabi asked leveling his laser pistol at Lucus. "I am not a patient man, if I don't get what I came for, you will all pay." He pointed his pistol at each of the crew and looked each in the eye. "Is that clear?"

They nodded, then Tom raised his pistol and fired at Zabi missing over his right shoulder. Zabi ducked returning fire and barely missed Tom who dropped behind a chair. Lucus fired at Al, but he had ducked behind a console and Lucus' shot hit the bulkhead behind him.

Bove fell to the floor along with Jack and Lucy

as Al fired over his head burning a console behind him.

"Stop!" shouted Luke, we only want the girl, there's no need for this."

"Okay," Lucus raised his hands and stood up behind the console. "Forgive my colleague for acting without my authority." He nodded at Tom, "We mean no harm. We'll give you the girl just as soon as we have her."

"Not good enough," Zabi said and fired a shot through Lucus blowing him back against the bulkhead. His pistol flew from his hand and slid across the floor stopping in front of the console where Jack knelt. Jack picked it up.

"No!" Shouted Tom standing up. He fired at Luke burning through his shoulder. Luke fell back against the bulkhead with a shout of pain and slid down into a sitting position.

Bove stood up and pointed his pistol at Zabi, hoping Jack would do the same. He did, pointing at Al. Tom kept his pistol trained on Luke who sat on the floor not moving. They held Zabi, Al, and Luke at bay. "Drop your weapons and get off this ship," Bove said, "before we blow you off."

Zabi glared at Bove. "Do you know who you're dealing with?" He raised his pistol toward Bove, but before it was level with Bove's body, Bove fired over Zabi's right shoulder.

"Your next move will come with a shot through your head." Bove held steady, eyes locked with Zabi.

Zabi nodded to Al, and they lowered their weapons to the floor. "Al, get Luke," he looked at Bove with a sneer on his face, "We'll be getting the girl soon enough. And you will pay for this. Believe me." With that Zabi backed out from the bridge. Bove followed with Jack and Tom supporting him.

They descended to the shuttle bay keeping pistols ready while Zabi boarded his shuttle. The minute they undocked, Bove touched the intercom to the bridge and said, "Lucy, Transit." And they were gone.

Twenty-Eight

"Whoa," Jack exclaimed, "that was intense!"

"Yeah?" Tom grabbed Bove by the throat and slammed him against the airlock door. "What the hell was that?" he demanded, pushing his laser pistol into Bove's gut. "You just lost us fifty thousand credits!"

"I had no choice," Bove coughed and twisted his head to relieve the pressure on his throat.

"You could have left well enough alone and let us collect our fifty grand, but no, you had to interfere." Tom pushed harder. "You know they'll be after us and won't stop until they get what they want!" He pushed again. "You know that don't you?" Tom glared into Bove's eyes, his grip tightening.

Bove coughed and slammed his right fist into Tom's solar plexus.

"Uff..." Tom grasped releasing his grip.

Bove reached out with his left hand and twisted the pistol from Tom's hand while pushing him away. "Like I said, I had no choice," he watched Tom try to get a breath as he stumbled back, falling to his knees.

Jack pressed himself against the lift door eyes like saucers as disbelief flooded his face. Tom had always been the force behind Lucus, the reason everyone stayed in line. If Lucus wanted something done, Tom made sure it happened. None of the crew defied him when he spoke.

"They're going to kill Stella," Bove said. "And I can't let that happen."

Tom gasped and coughed, "What are you talking about? You can't let that happen."

"I just can't. Let it go."

"I'm going to check on Lucy," Jack pressed the lift button and stepped in without looking back.

"Yeah," Bove glanced at him. "Let me know how she is, and Dan too."

Tom shook his head, took a deep breath, and said, "What are you doing? They're going to chase us until they get Stella."

"Like I said, I have no choice." Bove watched Tom's reaction.

"They'll kill us all; you know that don't you?" He glared at Bove.

"They can try," Bove stepped back and shoved Tom's pistol in his waistband. "But now we have more important things to discuss. Like, are you with us, or are you going to try and stop us?" He pointed his laser pistol at Tom, "If you're with us I'll need some confirmation. If not, I'll drop you at the nearest port."

Tom, still on his knees but breathing better, mumbled, "I only want my credits. Give me that and I'll be gone."

"Yeah," Bove said, "You only want credits, you don't care about anything else?"

"Yes, I care, but there's nothing we can do. Give them the girl and we can still get our credits."

"You think so?" Bove looked at Tom doubled over holding his stomach, "After what they did to Lucus? They'll kill us all given the chance, you must realize that." Bove studied Tom's pale face.

Tom nodded, "Yeah, I guess you're right." He took a deep breath, then another.

"There're more ways to get credits, honorable ways. And we can get them. So, are you with us? Or do I drop you at the next port?"

Tom nodded, "Do I have a choice?"

"Yeah, you do," Bove answered. "I just told you—stay or leave at the next port."

Tom looked at Bove then nodded, "Yeah, okay. If you can get the credits I lost…"

"Fair enough," Bove cut him off. "But first we have to get Stella safe and out of this situation, so are you with us on that?"

Tom nodded taking another breath. "Yeah," he said.

"Come on," Bove said holding out his hand to help Tom to his feet.

Tom accepted Bove's gesture and stood up. "What now?" he asked.

"We find out what's really going on, so if you know it would be a great booster to my confidence." Bove studied his eyes for a reaction.

Tom glanced away. "I don't know, Lucus kept everything to himself. He told me her family wanted her back and these guys were going to deliver her, so I didn't ask questions."

"That's it?"

"Yeah, he said all her talk about being killed was to get me to sympathize with her, so I blew it off."

Stupid, Bove thought then said, "Well, we're going to find out what's really going on, and I don't think those guys were going to give her back to her family, do you?"

Tom shook his head, "I guess not."

"Okay, then let's go." Bove punched deck three in the lift keeping Tom safely against the opposite side. When they arrived at deck three Bove opened the door to the cabin where Stella was hiding. He looked around then said softly, "Stella."

She looked over the side of the bed pointing the rifle at him.

"It's me, Bove," Bove said holding up his hands with no weapon showing.

"Who's with you?" Stella asked.

"Tom, but it's okay. I've talked to him and he's with us."

"Do you have weapons?" she asked.

"I do," Bove held up his hands, weapon-free, "but Tom doesn't. It's safe."

Stella's eyes scanned back and forth at each of them. She stood up still holding the rifle pointed at Tom. "Show me your hands," she said.

Tom raised his hands. "Look," he said. "I'm sorry for the trouble, I was doing what Lucus told me to do."

"Well, you should think for yourself." Stella raised her rifle level with Tom's head, "Are you still doing what you're told?"

Tom shook his head. "No, I'm doing what's right."

"And what's that?"

"Finding what's really going on. Why you're wanted by those guys."

"I'll tell you why." Stella lowered her weapon but kept it pointed at Tom. "I stole their shipment, and they want it back."

"Shipment of what?" Bove asked.

"Weapons," she said.

"Well, they are weapons dealers," Tom glanced at Stella.

"Why would you do that?" Bove asked.

"Their weapons were headed for the rebels on my home world. There's a revolution going on that the rebels are winning. And with a new supply of weapons, they would have the advantage to win the war. We would be enslaved by them."

"Why is there a revolution? Is your government suppressing the people, overtaxing them, taking away their rights?"

"No!" Stella glared at Bove. "No, they're giving everyone rights to do as they wish. Making everyone equal under the law, and the rebels don't want that. The rebels believe only the educated should have the right to vote new leaders in, and only the rich should have the right to education. They want only the rich to rule the land and everyone else to bow before them."

"Yeah? So, you took the weapons?"

"Yeah, I took them. I want them for the government. With additional weapons, we should be able to turn the war in our favor."

"So, you're a soldier?" Bove asked.

"Not really, I've worked in law enforcement for a while, but not a soldier."

"How did you know Zabi's weapons were for the rebels?"

"I have my sources. Like I said I've worked in law enforcement for a while, and I've made contacts. They know stuff, they tell me stuff."

"Like who has weapons and for whom?"

"Yeah," Stella looked at Tom slightly raising her rifle. "What do you have to say?"

"Nothing," Tom said. "I'm in it for the credits,

nothing more."

"Great," Stella turned to Bove. "You trust him?"

"We'll see when the chips are down," Bove said.

"What now? And where are we?" Stella asked.

"Don't know," Bove said, "Not in the Tau-Ceti System, I had us transited out."

"Yeah, I noticed."

"You want the weapons." Bove studied her reaction.

She flinched. "Yeah, that's what I said. Are we going back for them?"

"I don't know. Where are they?"

"In the asteroid belt in the Tau-Ceti System."

"We just came from there and Zabi's there waiting for us. I don't think we should go back there." Tom said.

"Then get me someplace I can catch a ride back. I am going to get those weapons."

"Okay," Bove said. "Just hold on a minute. Let me figure out where we are and what our status is. Tom come with me, Stella you can come or stay here."

Bove left herding Tom in front of him. Stella followed keeping her rifle pointed at Tom.

They made their way to the bridge. Lucus still lay where he had fallen. Lucy was sitting at her console focused totally on her screen. Jack was checking his console and glancing at Lucy from time to time. Dan was nowhere in sight. Tom stopped at the door staring at Lucus' body, all his force seemed to have left him, he sighed and leaned against the wall dazed.

Stella stepped into the bridge after Tom. "So," she said looking at Lucus' body lying on the floor. "Who's in charge?"

Everyone looked at each other, then at Bove.

"This is your deal, Bove," Jack said. "So, what do we do now?"

"Where are we?" Bove asked.

"Vega," Jack said.

"Any chance Zabi can trace us?"

"No."

"Okay, here's the deal. Stella's world is in the middle of a revolution against her government by a faction that wants to enslave everyone. They want to put the rich in power and suppress everyone else. The weapons she stole were destined for the rebels and would tip the war in their favor. Stella wants the weapons for her government to change the tide of the war to their favor."

"And you learned this from her?" Jack pointed at Stella.

Bove nodded.

"And you are taking her word without any proof?"

"We'll get proof."

"How?"

"We're going to her world and ask the government what's going on."

Dan came in the main door to the bridge, "Who's world?" he asked.

Bove turned toward him glancing over his body. He didn't need someone taking sides with Lucus' memory. So, he wanted to be sure Dan wasn't carrying a weapon. He appeared clean. Bove turned back to Jack.

"You think that's wise?" Jack looked at Bove then Lucy and Tom for support. "Tom?"

Tom looked up, shook his head, "I think we

need to get out of this. There's no chance of getting our credits and if we go back there's a good chance Zabi will get us. I don't want to even think about that. We need to cut our losses."

"What about Stella," Lucy asked.

"Dump her at the next port. Let her fight her own battles. After all, it's not our revolution or our concern." Tom looked at Stella. "She's nothing but trouble."

Stella raised her rifle, "Maybe I'll trouble you," she said.

"Stella," Bove reached out and pushed her rifle down. "Enough! We're trying to figure a way to help you out."

She looked at him, then Tom, who raised his hands, palms out. "Yeah, okay."

"Where's your home world?" Bove asked.

"Ceti-2," Stella said.

"Oh shit," Tom said.

"Great," Jack said.

"What?" Dan dropped into his chair.

Lucy sighed and put her head in her hands leaning on her console.

Bove rubbed his head and sat down, "Ceti-2?" he asked

Stella nodded.

"What now?" Jack asked.

"Where in the asteroid belt are the weapons?" Bove asked.

"Well, it's hard to explain, but they're on one of the largest asteroids close to the outer rim. I can guide you there easier than telling you."

"Jack, can we get back in there without Zabi detecting us?"

"I don't know. It depends on what he has on his ship. From what I saw of it I would guess he has the latest equipment and if so, then yes, he can track us. Within minutes of entering the system, he'll spot us."

"Can we avoid him somehow?"

"I can see if a deflection shield will work," Lucy said. "It won't last very long because there're ways to detect it with good sensors, but it will work for a while."

"Long enough to get in and out?"

"A day or so," Lucy said.

"What are you thinking?" Jack asked.

Bove turned to him, paused, and looked at each of them, Jack, Lucy, Dan, then Tom. "Okay," he said, "I have to do whatever is necessary to prevent harm coming to anyone."

"What do you mean you have to do what's necessary?" Tom asked, eyes open in surprise. "You don't have to do anything."

"Yes, I do," Bove answered. "And I have to do it whether any of you are with me or not. Maybe someday I'll explain, but right now we have to deal with what's before us, and that's Stella. So, what I'm proposing is that we go back get the weapons and stop at her world to judge the situation for ourselves."

"And let Zabi take Stella and kill us because that's what he's going to do," Tom spoke up.

Dan turned his seat to see everyone, face pale and hands shaking.

"We'll see about that. There're ways to tip the odds to our favor," Bove said.

Twenty-Nine

An hour later they had a plan. Stella had pinpointed the asteroid, explained the situation on Ceti-2 and what to expect when they arrived. The plan was to transit to the asteroid belt, retrieve the weapons, go to Ceti-2 to verify Stella's story, and deliver her and the weapons, then get out of the system. All that remained was to set up to transit.

Bove stood up, looked at Stella then Jack. "Take us in away from Zabi. If he spots us it'll take him a day or two to reach us."

"Unless he transits across." Jack punched buttons and checked his screen.

"No one's that stupid; he'd destroy himself," Tom declared. "He won't take the chance,"

"How close will we be to the weapons?" Bove looked at Stella sitting behind him in the captain's seat.

"Not far," she said. "Maybe half a day into the asteroids."

"Our shields will hide us for a day before we're detected—right?" Bove glanced at Lucy.

"Yeah," she said. "Maybe a day and a half."

"Okay, once we have the weapons, we'll head for Ceti-2 at top speed. Two days, right Jack?"

"If everything goes smoothly," Jack said.

"Lucy, can you vary the shield frequency to

hide us for another day, or so?" Bove watched the uncertainty flicker across her face. "We need a buffer if it takes longer."

"I'll see what I can do." She shook her head.

"Let me know when we're ready. I'm going to get some rest. Jack, you're in charge. Keep these two," Bove nodded toward Tom and Stella, "away from each other."

Jack looked at Bove shaking his head slightly. Bove turned to Stella locking eyes "Give Jack the rifle."

"Not on your life," Stella glared at him, then glanced at Tom.

"Jack's in charge. Tom won't do anything, right Tom?"

"Yeah," Tom glared at Stella, "if she doesn't."

"Stella," Bove said.

"Yeah, okay." She handed the rifle to Jack. "But if he tries anything…"

"Yeah, Yeah," Bove interrupted and left the bridge thinking about their next move. Getting to the asteroid belt would not be a problem but loading the weapons and getting to Ceti-2 is another issue. By the time they get to the weapons Zabi will know where they are and be on his way to reach them. *It'll be close*, Bove thought. *If Zabi gets to us before we're done, we'll have to fight. We need to avoid that at all costs.*

Zabi's ship had greater firepower and is faster than the Ibex, so they needed something to even the odds. But what? *What about weapons…* Bove thought, *the ship has three blasters, two in front and one in back. We have hand weapons—two pistols and a rifle. If we can keep Zabi off the ship, we have a chance. I wonder how fast this ship is… Could we out-run him? Doubtful.*

217

Bove lay on his bunk closed his eyes and let his thoughts drift. Why had he taken this job? It felt wrong from the start, but he had pushed that aside because he needed the work. He was going nuts not being able to do something; he had to keep busy. And this job was his only option, or was there something else? Had he taken it because of Stella? Had he somehow known she was in trouble? Some universal string pulling at him to do the right thing? *No, there's no way.* Did Tanka have something to do with this? *Is he guiding me to situations that need intervention? Am I a pawn in some cosmic game the Krytheons are playing? Are they testing me?*

Bove's eyes slid shut as he drifted with his thoughts into a world of dreams. In his dream world, he was in a forest of giant trees towering hundreds of meters above him. He stepped to one and was standing on a platform high in the branches looking down on a shuttle sitting in a clearing below.

They have come, the man standing next to him said, *and they will never leave. Our world has changed forever.*

Bove turned toward but no one was there. Who has come? Bove wondered, then saw below men in uniforms stepping from the shuttle. They looked up into the trees but never saw Bove hidden among the leaves. Then voices came to him, clear in the still air, *The teams all agreed this was good for colonization, and they were right. It's beautiful, an Eden.*

Bove stepped back taking a deep breath and sat up in his bunk. "What," he said looking around the cabin. He was alone. *Just a dream*, he thought then realized he had another decision like the one on Kryth, a decision that would change the lives of everyone on

Ceti-2. And he had to do something to make that happen.

The intercom crackled, "Bove," Lucy cut into his thoughts, "we're ready."

Bove rubbed his head and face, lay back for a minute. *Okay*, he thought, *I have to do this, but they don't have to do it with me. I need to tell them they can go. They have a choice.*

He headed to the bridge to find everyone working in silence. Lucus' body was gone although there was still evidence where he had been shot. "Where's Lucus?" He asked.

"We put him in his office," Jack looked up at Bove. "We need to take care of him if you know what I mean."

Bove nodded. Lucy and Tom turned toward him, waiting. He rubbed his face and sat in the pilot's seat.

"So," Stella said, "what's the deal? Do we shove him out the airlock, stick him in the freezer? What?"

"Shit!" Tom jumped to his feet. "You don't have to be so crass, do you?" He glared at Stella. "Maybe we should shove you out the airlock."

"Enough!" Bove shouted standing up and confronting both Stella and Tom. "We'll give him a funeral, show him a little respect. Is that ok with everyone?"

"Whatever," Stella shrugged.

"I swear I'll throw you out the airlock," Tom stepped toward Stella.

"Just try," She stood facing him.

"Enough!" Bove roared. "Sit down. Tom step back. We are going to give Lucus a proper funeral and a burial in space. And that's the end of it. Understood?"

He glared at both Stella and Tom.

Tom stepped back nodding. Stella lowered into her chair. "Yeah, whatever," she said.

Bove turned to Jack, Dan, and Lucy who all nodded and turned back to their stations without a word.

"Good," Bove said. "Let's do it."

The funeral was short. Tom talked about how Lucus had always tried to do good for his crew. Always had *making a profit* for each of them his prime objective.

Dan said he always had their backs. His crew was his most important asset, and he couldn't do anything without them. He talked about the times they almost had the big score, but never quite made it.

Lucy said "Good-by Lucus."

Jack had nothing to say.

They had wrapped his body in a tarp and laid him in the loading bay. After each had their say, they moved to the control room and opened the cargo bay doors. Lucus' body ejected out with the rush of air into the vacuum of space.

Stella said, "Good riddance."

Tom raised his fist, "You Bit…"

Bove pushed his fist down, "Stop. It's over. Let it go."

"It'll be over when we're rid of that bitch," Tom said. Then walked away.

Stella raised her fist like an uppercut to Tom's back.

Bove glared at her, "Enough." He pressed the button to close the cargo bay door.

They returned to the bridge where Stella promptly took the captain's seat. Tom just glared at her.

"So," he said.

"You're in the captain's chair." Bove promptly interjected looking at Tom then Stella.

"That's for you," Lucy pointed toward the captain's chair.

"We discussed it," Jack said, "you're in charge."

"Okay, for now," Bove nodded at the crew. "But once we're done with this we'll see. Which brings up another subject. I have to do this. I have to get Stella back to her world, but you don't. You have a choice. I can take you anywhere you want. Once this is over, if I still have control of the ship, I will bring it back to you. To whoever wants it. So, what I'm saying is that if you want out, speak up."

He looked at each of them waiting for their reaction.

Jack spoke first, "I've been on this ship for the last four years and this is the first time we're doing something to help someone instead of to get more credits. Not that the credits aren't good, but still, credits aren't everything. I'm staying."

Bove looked at Tom.

Tom shrugged and shook his head. "Lucus and I were together for six years. We'd been through everything, but he never made the big score he talked about. I guess he never would have. It's all about the credits you know, and you took that away from me, from us." He looked at Jack, Dan, and Lucy, then back to Bove. "But I don't have any place else to be. This has been my home, so to speak, so I guess I'm in. Who knows maybe there's a reward for saving Stella."

"You trust him," Lucy asked.

"Can I?" Bove looked directly at Tom. "If not, I can always turn you over to Zabi."

"You can trust me." Tom looked at Dan then Jack and Lucy. "If you don't, just drop me at the nearest port."

"I'll think about that," Bove said.

"Sounds good to me," Stella interjected.

Bove nodded to Tom, glared at Stella, then turned to Lucy, "Do you want to be taken someplace?"

She shook her head, "No, I have no place to go. I'll help you get Stella home "

"And after?" Bove asked.

"Well, let's see if there is an after," she said.

"What about you, Dan. Are you staying or not?"

"I have no other prospects and no place to go. I'll help."

"So," Bove said, "everyone's in? I'm surprised. I don't know if I would stay if I had the choice."

"You do," Lucy said.

"Not really." Bove looked at the crew. His crew, it seemed, at least for now. "Okay," he said. "Are we ready to transit?"

"Give me a minute," Jack said. "I want to be sure of our arrival point."

"Okay, you'll put us as close to the asteroid as you can?"

"Sure," Jack nodded and turned to his console.

"Everything working?" Bove looked at Lucy.

Lucy nodded, "All the parameters are set, and I've taken care of the engines for you."

Jack and Lucy checked their consoles.

"Stella, once we're at the asteroid how long will it take to load everything?" Bove asked.

"Do you have a tractor lift?"

"Two in the cargo bay." Bove turned to Tom. "Are they operational?"

"Yeah."

"Okay," Bove looked back at Stella. "How long?"

"It took me a day with a tractor lift to move them into the cave."

"A day, huh?" Bove mused. "Okay." He turned back to Tom, "That work for you?"

"With Dan's help, we can do it in half the time."

Bove looked at Dan, who nodded, then Stella. "Okay," he said. "We'll transit when everything's ready." He turned to Lucy. "Lucy," she looked up and turned to face him. "Can you set up to transit by yourself?"

"Yeah, but it'll take two and a half, maybe three hours."

"Okay, once we're in the system get to work on a transit. We may need it."

Lucy looked at Bove questions running across her face. She glanced toward Jack who looked as bewildered as her. "Okay," she turned back to her console.

"Dan," Bove looked at Dan who turned to face him. "What's your job?"

"I kinda know everything there is to know about the ship."

"Like what?"

"I make sure everything's working, computers are up and running, engines, and life support are functioning correctly, sensors are working. You know, pretty much everything."

"The weapons?"

"Yeah, the blasters too."

"Tell me about them."

"Not much to tell. There're two blasters in the

front and one in the back."

"That's it?"

"Yeah."

"What's their power and range?"

"Power's 50K mega wats and each has a range of four thousand meters, but at that distance, you'll be lucky to hit anything. These blasters are for blowing rocks out of the way. If there's a big object in the way they're great for getting rid of it."

"A big object, like a spaceship?" Bove looked at Dan a slight smile creasing his lips.

Dan nodded, "Yeah, I guess so."

"Okay, then," Bove said. "Jack, Lucy, what's the status?"

"We're ready," Jack said.

"Everyone secure?" The crew nodded.

Stella said, "Secure."

"Transit." Bove closed his eyes and wondered what they were headed for.

*   *   *

They came into the far edge of the Tau-Ceti system, at the edge of the asteroid belt, and a day, or two from the weapons. There was no indication of any ships nearby, no indication of any detection by Zabi, and everything looked good.

"Jack, give us a map of the system." Bove looked at the main view screen.

Jack pressed a couple of buttons and the main viewer turned into a map of the Tau-Ceti system. A green light flashed indicating their location in the asteroid belt and a red light showed Zabi's last location outside the orbit of Ceti-4.

"Jack, isolate the asteroid belt." The viewscreen changed showing the asteroid belt. "Locate Stella's asteroid." A short distance from the edge of the belt a blue light blinked on.

"Is that it?" Jack turned to Stella still sitting in the captain's chair. She nodded.

"How long to get there?" Bove asked.

"Uh, from here, thirty-four hours."

"Get us there as fast as you can. Lucy, how long can you keep us hidden?"

"A little over a day."

"So, we're going to be visible before we get there. Jack how long for Zabi to reach us?"

"If he's still where we left him it'll take him seventy-five hours."

"Good, we'll be well on our way to Ceti-2 by then. He'll have some catching up to do." Bove sat and considered their situation, they had a head start. Zabi was far across the system and unable to reach them before they could get the weapons and be on their way to Ceti-2. Yes, it looked like they could pull this off without a problem.

"Dan," he said. "Show me what the blasters can do, how they operator, and what they can hit."

Dan turned his chair to the console on his left. "They're controlled from here," he pointed to the controls. "There's a set for the forward blasters, here, and one for the rear. They fire a blast up to four thousand meters and can blow apart a good size rock. The rear has the same power and range. You can't target anything. They fire straight ahead or behind, nothing to the side. You need to place the ship in the path of whatever you want to hit." Dan looked over his shoulder at Bove, who nodded. "To fire them use these controls." He pointed to the left set of controls. "This one will set the power, this one the range, and this will fire the blaster, the same for the rear blaster. Pretty simple."

"Humm," Bove mused. "We use the ship to target and have to be within four thousand meters, got it."

"Well," Dan looked up at Bove, "If you want to actually hit anything, you'll need to be within two thousand meters. Sorry."

"Two?" Bove shook his head.

"Yeah, that way you can be more accurate."

"Good to know, thanks." Bove turned towards Jack and Lucy. "Tomorrow we'll be ready to get the weapons. And Zabi will be nowhere near us." He wrinkled his brow as an uneasy feeling pressed in on him. "Let's get some rest."

Everyone gave an uncertain nod then headed out. Stella lagged and when the bridge was clear she asked, "What's your plan if Zabi boards?"

"He won't." Bove stepped towards the door.

"But if he does?" Stella raised her voice. "What then?"

Bove turned toward her with a smile on his face. "Like I said, he won't. We'll make sure he doesn't do anything to allow that."

"And how will you do that?"

"I have my ways; Okay?"

"No, this is my neck we're talking about, and vague comments about protecting me doesn't cut it. I want some assurance."

"Zabi won't be able to get to us before we have the weapons loaded and we're on our way. Okay?"

"You think so?"

"I know so. Now get some rest."

"You're sure?"

"Yes."

Stella looked uncertain but nodded. "Where do I sleep?"

"Where I had you before, cabin six."

*   *   *

Zabi checked his console and leaned back with a smile. "They're back," he said. "With some inadequate shields to hide behind."

"What's the plan, go after them?" Luke asked.

"They've come back for the weapons. All we have to do is wait. When they get to them, we'll transit."

"Into the asteroid belt?" Sam almost yelled.

"No, you idiot!" Zabi glared at him. "To the edge of the belt."

"We'll still be a day away." Al pointed out.

"Doesn't matter. It's going to take them two days to load everything onto their ship. We'll surprise 'em and take what's ours. Then we'll kill them all." Zabi thought for a moment, "except the girl. I want her. Is that understood?"

"Yeah," the crew said together.

"Good, now keep track of them and let me know when they're to the shipment."

"We'll get our credits then?" Carter asked.

"Yeah, we'll get our credits."

"And the girl? When you're done?" Carter asked.

"You want her?" Zabi studied Carter, "You can have her. Then she goes out the airlock."

"Yeah, sure."

"That's quick," Luke said, "Maybe do her slower. After all she did take our shipment and that deserves a long slow punishment, don't you think?"

"Yeah," Carter agreed. "When we're done with

227

her maybe we should cut her up. A piece at a time."

"Yeah," Luke smiled and ran his tongue over his lips. "Start with her fingers and work up."

"You're all gross," Ruby said. "Just slit her throat and be done with it."

"No, no, no!" Zabi yelled. "I don't want to soil my ship with her blood. We'll toss her out the airlock and that's final."

The crew nodded and mumbled disagreement under their breath, which Zabi ignored. "Good," his lip curled up in satisfaction.

Thirty

Noon the following day the Ibex arrived at Stella's asteroid. "Take it slow," Bove said as they approached, "Slow and easy."

"All systems are optimum," Lucy said.

"Where are the weapons?" Bove turned to Stella.

"They're in a cave. Go around. We'll find it."

"We better, we don't have much time." He glanced at Lucy then Jack, "Any sign of Zabi?"

"Not that I can see," Lucy answered. "The shields seem to be doing their job." She leaned back in her seat smiling.

"Good, you see anything?" Bove asked Jack.

"Nope," Jack studied his console. "It looks like Zabi hasn't moved; guess he hasn't spotted us."

Bove steered the ship around the asteroid watching the surface as they passed over it. "Do you see it?" he asked Stella.

"Not yet. It's close though."

They continued around the asteroid slowly scanning the surface for any sign of the cave. Sensors studied the surface sending back detailed information on the terrain, but nothing like what Stella described. They continued.

"I'm picking up some interference with our

shields," Lucy commented casually.

"What kind of interference?" Bove asked.

"Just a fluctuation in the wave pattern, nothing to worry about."

Bove thought about that. He had seen fluctuations before caused by sensor probes to the sensors. *Could this be the same?* He wondered then put it out of his mind. There were more important things to worry about right now, like finding the cave with the weapons. Then again fluctuations are caused by something, "Lucy, check on Zabi, see if he's moved."

"He's still where he was. I don't think he knows we're here."

"Okay."

"I'm getting some variances on the surface," Jack said, "looks like some hills."

"That's it," Stella said jumping up and gazing at the viewscreen. "Yeah, that's it. That's where I stashed them, right there in that cave. See it?"

Bove looked at the view screen and studied the terrain until he finally saw a cave. "Zoom in," he told Jack. The scene zoomed to an area around the cave showing tracks from a tractor lift running into the hillside. "Okay," he said, "Let's go down and see what's there. Tom, you're with me and Stella. Get suited up and be ready in fifteen."

Bove turned to Dan, "You're coming too," he said.

"You're going to need both shuttles. There're about two hundred and fifty crates." Stella sat up straight in the captain's chair.

"What?" Bove stared at her. "Two hundred and fifty? Change of plans. Dan, you, and Tom get a lift on each shuttle. We'll take both down."

In the shuttle bay, Tom and Dan manipulated the tractor lifts into the shuttle's cargo bays through the loading door at the back of each shuttle. Once they were secure, they suited up and boarded.

Bove checked that the shuttles were sealed and ready for departure. He opened the bay doors to reveal rough gray pitted rock that made up the asteroid's surface and appeared to be no more than ten meters below them. He accelerated forward out the bay doors towards the surface where they settled down about twenty meters from the cave entrance. "Everyone secure," he asked.

"Yeah." Dan and Stella answered as they released their restraining belts.

Tom's shuttle settled down next to Bove's.

"Okay." The shuttle view screen revealed the harsh terrain of the asteroid, "They better be here," Bove released his restraining belt and stood up. "We don't have a lot of time to go exploring."

"It's right," Stella said, "The weapons are about fifty meters inside."

"Are they going to fit on the shuttles?" He asked.

Stella and Dan looked at each other, "I have no idea," Dan said,

Stella shrugged, "Probably not," she shook her head.

"Great!" Bove pushed past Stella to the exit. "Open the cargo door," he said to Dan and headed out.

Once outside the shuttle, he saw Tom driving the tractor lift out of the cargo bay. He switched his communicator to Tom's channel, "Tom, are those crates going to fit in the shuttle?"

"Not likely," Tom sent back. "I'll have a look at

them to get a good estimate."

"OK, do it.": Bove looked back for Stella. She was standing at the top of the cargo ramp.

"Dan," Bove said, "get the lift out of the shuttle. We're going to check the cave." He waved to Tom to follow.

Tom and Stella followed Bove into the cave, Stella directing them to the weapons. About forty meters in were the crates. There were assorted sizes and stacked on pallets three to four high; some so large the lift would have to take a few crates at a time.

"Okay." Bove scanned the crates getting a rough estimate of the trips it would take to get them to the Ibex. "What'd you think Tom?"

Tom walked around the stacks glancing up and down. "Two hundred and fifty crates. It's going to take several trips. We should be able to finish by tomorrow."

"Tom, you and Dan, start getting the crates into the shuttles. Stella get 'em organized to fit the cargo bays. I'm going to check on Lucy and Jack.

In the shuttle Bove radioed Jack. "What's the status?"

"Lucy's picked up a transit disturbance at the edge of the ring."

Bove felt a tightening in his gut. Someone had transited close by, and there was only one person that would do that. "How far are they?"

"About a day away." Jack's voice had a slight tremble to it.

"Great!" Bove disconnected and headed out to see how the loading was going. Crates were loaded into the shuttle and lifters were heading back to get more. Stella was going between shuttles to determine where the next load should go. A couple of palates were sitting on the ground next to each shuttle waiting for the right place to insert them.

Bove switched his radio on and connected to everyone. "We have a problem. Zabi has transited to the edge of the belt."

"What?" Stella's voice was sharp. "How close is he?"

Bove heard the lifts stop and silence drifted across the communications as everyone waited for the answer. "About a day away," he said.

"We had better step it up." Tom started his lifter and rumbled ahead of Dan who followed.

"We're not leaving any of these weapons." Stella was facing Bove, but he only saw his reflection in her visor. He could tell from the tone of her voice she was deadly serious. "We'll get then all." Again, deadly serious.

He ignored her and watched the two lifters come out of the cave each carrying a pallet of crates.

"Stella, get that one loaded. I'll do this one."

They had to leave enough room to load the lifter after the crates were in the shuttle. Once that was done, they went to the Ibex and unloaded, then returned for another load. On each trip, they were able to carry eighteen to twenty crates in each shuttle and it took three to four hours to get the shuttle loaded and unloaded in the Ibex.

Late that night they flew up with the final load. They left it in the shuttles and headed to the bridge where all four fell into their seats exhausted.

"Set an itinerary to Ceti-2 for maximum speed," Bove told Jack. "And go the minute you're ready." He lay his head against the back of his seat and closed his eyes wishing he was in his cabin ready for a night's rest.

The radio cracked and Zabi's voice came into the bridge, "This is the Dark Star demanding the stolen weapons you have just retrieved. That shipment belongs to us and if they are not returned immediately, we will take them by force. You have fifteen minutes to comply."

The radio fell silent as did the bridge on the Ibex.

"Lucy," Bove turned to her, "are we ready to transit?"

"Not quite. With everything going on I haven't been able to finish setting up."

"How long?"

"With Jack's help, another twenty minutes."

"Twenty minutes?"

"Forty if I do it alone. With the fluctuations in the shields and keeping the ship over the cave I haven't had much time," she snapped. "I'll get on it."

Stella shifted in the captain's chair, "I'm sorry I got you into this."

"It's too late for that," Tom said, "Zabi wants the weapons and he'll do anything to get them, including destroying the ship."

"That will lose him the weapons," Jack turned and looked at Tom.

"He'll board the ship with more help than last time," Tom shot back.

"No, he won't," Bove said, "Turn the ship to face him head-on.

"What?" Jack strengthened in his seat, "Shouldn't we get out of here?"

"We can't outrun him and if we try, he'll fire on us, probably disable the ship for boarding. He won't destroy us until he has the weapons. That gives us an advantage."

"How so?" Tom asked.

"Turn to him," Bove instructed Jack.

Jack turned the ship facing Zabi directly, "Okay, now what?"

"Let's see what he does," Bove sat up in the pilot's chair.

The bridge fell into a deathly silence as everyone watched the viewscreen displaying the Dark Star sitting a mere eight thousand meters away.

"Give him the weapons," Tom said.

"No," Stella jumped out of the captain's chair. "You can't do that, they're for the rebels and it will change the course of the war." Her eyes bore into Tom. "The rebels are already threatening to take over the capital and once that happens there's no hope. Those weapons will tilt the war in their favor. You can't give them to him!"

"We're not going to," Bove said. "Not only do I have to help you; I have to help your world." He stood up, turned to face his crew, then asked, "Are you still with me?"

The silence returned like heavy air pressing on everyone. Bove felt a chill run through him.

"We don't have any choice," Tom said. "If we try to leave Zabi will shoot us out of space. We have to stay."

"That's not the question, will you back me?"

"Yes," Jack looked at each crew member. "We'll back you. We already decided that. Get with it," he said looking at Tom.

Bove nodded. "Lucy," he said. "Can you determine anything about their ship, where their weapon controls are, life support, engines, anything that can give us an advantage?"

"I don't know, this is quite a sophisticated ship, top of the line. It has everything. I don't know how they detected us. They have shields keeping our sensors from penetrating, but I think I can bypass that and get something for you. Give me a couple of minutes."

"We don't have a couple of minutes," Tom sounded defeated.

"We have twelve," Lucy shot back.

Bove thought it through, they are facing a powerful ship, but the crew is not well trained. They do things by brute force. They showed that by boarding the ship last time. They didn't know what was waiting for them, but they boarded anyway. Now they know the crew size and our weapons status. They still don't know what we can do with this ship.

"Got it," Lucy said. "Everything's linked to their main system which is located behind the bridge."

"Everything?" Bove asked.

"Yeah, their weapons, life support, navigation, everything."

"Dan, can we target that?"

"Not from here."

"From where?"

"We'll need to be under four thousand meters."

"And you said to hit anything we need to be at two thousand. Right?"

"Yeah, the blasters will shoot four, but they aren't accurate. You'll have to be within a thousand for that kind of accuracy."

"Jack, can you get us there? How long do we have?"

"Four minutes," Lucy said.

"Dan get those blasters ready to fire I'll get us lined up." Bove dropped into the pilot's chair.

"They'll know the minute we power the blasters," Dan's voice quivered, and sweat beaded on his forehead.

"Then power them now. We'll deal with their response."

"No!" Dan pushed up out of his chair and stepped away from the console, "They'll fire on us. They'll destroy us!"

"Dan!" Bove stood up glaring at him, "you said you were with us, which means you do as I say. Is that clear?"

Dan hesitated, backed into his console, his face turned pale. "If we power weapons, they'll fire on us. They'll blow us out of space."

"No, they won't. They want the weapons, and they'll not do anything to harm them until they're on the Dark Star. When we power, they will too, but they won't fire."

Bove stared into Dan's eyes until Dan lowered his head.

"Okay" he mumbled and with shaking hands he sat.

"Once weapons are powered hold off firing until I give you the word." Bove sat back in his seat. "Tell me when they're ready."

"Weapons are powered," Dan said thirty seconds later.

"Have they powered?"

"Not yet."

Bove shifted in his chair and started the ship slowly moving toward the Dark Star.

He activated the radio. "Dark Star." he looked at

his crew, "we are coming with the weapons." Not a lie, they were coming with the weapons, just not to deliver them, but then Zabi did not need to know that.

Once they were within a thousand meters, they should be able to disable the Dark Star's weapons. With the weapons down they should have enough time to make a break for Ceti-2. If this failed, it would take skilled flying to get away from them.

"Seven thousand meters," Jack announced.

"Dan, are you ready?"

"When you are," Dan ran a hand over his head and shifted in his seat.

"Jack, how long until we're at a thousand meters?"

"At this rate, thirty seconds."

"That's going to be a long thirty seconds," Lucy said.

"Six thousand meters," Jack said.

"Time left?" Bove asked.

"Two minutes," Lucy answered.

What will they do when our times up?" Dan looked over at Bove.

"Probably send a shuttle to board us," Tom said.

"Good, we'll wait."

Silence fell over the bridge leaving only the background noise of the engines pushing them toward the Dark Star. Seconds slid by as time slipped into the past. Soft breathing cut the silence marking the presence of life. The radio crackled to life startling everyone.

"Your time is up," announced Zabi. "Stop your advance and prepare to be boarded. Any resistance will be met with dire circumstances."

"Have they powered weapons?" Bove looked at

Dan.

"No," Dan said.

"How far are we?"

"Five thousand meters."

Bove kept the ship moving forward ignoring Zabi's threat. "Distance?" He asked Jack.

"Four thousand."

The radio crackled again. "I said, stop your advance. Prepare to be boarded."

Bove kept moving toward the Dark Star. "How far?"

"Twenty-five hundred," Jack said.

"Can you hit them?"

"Another five-hundred would be better." Dan's voice was calmer but still unsteady.

"Stop your advance now," Zabi said again.

"They've powered weapons."

"This will have to do."

Bove fired the retro thrusters causing the Ibex to slowly stop twenty-four hundred meters from the Dark Star. He focused on his console and the controls gauging the fine-tuning he needed to line up with the Dark Star's control center.

The radio crackled again, "Our weapons are locked on your ship. If you try to run, we will fire. Rest assured we won't destroy you only incapacitate your ship. Chances are no one will find you before your life support fails."

"Dan," Bove tapped his console controls. "Fire a burst from the forward blaster on my count."

Dan's face paled and his hands shook, and he spun around looking directly at Bove. "What are you doing? They'll blow us outa space!"

"Do It!" Bove glared at him. "Then hold onto

your seats. Jack, are we set for Ceti-2?"

"Yeah, but..." Jack turned back to his console checking his settings.

Bove watched the Dark Star while the shuttle exited the bay and began its approach to the Ibex. He estimated the distance to be about halfway between the ships when he checked the alignment and said, "Three..."

"Oh, no," Lucy shuttered.

"Two," Bove announced.

"Oh shit," Jack exclaimed.

"Fire," Bove commanded.

Dan fired and closed his eyes, "I hope there's a God."

Bove fired the thrusters at full power and turned to the left throwing the ship to the left and above the Dark Star. The Dark Star fired a return blast that flew under the Ibex barely grazing the underside as they flew over Zabi's ship. The Ibex's blaster hit the Dark Star right in the control center.

The Dark Star spun around and lined up with the Ibex but was unable to fire.

"Their weapons are down," Lucy cried.

The radio crackled, "You will pay for this," Zabi's anger blasted through the connection.

"Get us to Ceti-2," Bove yelled at Jack.

"You got it," Jack shouted punching in controls to direct them to Ceti-2.

"How much time before they're after us?" Bove asked,

"Once the shuttle is docked, they'll be on the way," Jack said. "We didn't do anything to their engines only their weapons."

"How long for their weapons to be up?"

"Five minutes," Dan said, "They have redundancy systems for everything. I'm surprised their weapons aren't already operational."

"Their shuttle's docked," Jack said, "They're coming."

"That's just great!" Bove turned the Ibex directly into the asteroid field, his focus totally on the guidance controls as rocks sped past them, nicking the hull.

"What are you doing?" Tom shouted at Bove.

"Getting us free from Zabi," Bove answered back.

The Ibex flew between the asteroids dodging the small ones and avoiding the larger ones with the Dark Star in pursuit, larger, faster, and better armed, but not as agile. The Ibex zipped around a large asteroid, slowed spinning at a tight angle, and slipped behind another. The Dark Star blasted around the first large asteroid, slowed turning slowly, and came to a full stop.

"It's pointless to run," Zabi said over the radio, "I'll find you no matter where you are. And you are close, are you not?"

"Lucy, can you get any reading on them?"

"No, they're behind a rock the sensors can't see through it."

"Can you bounce off something and get a reading?"

"Clever," Lucy studied her console intently. "You may be onto something. I got a fuzzy image."

"Put it on the viewer."

A fuzzy picture appeared on the viewer, it jiggled but showed the Dark Star sitting nearby behind a large asteroid. It was rotating slowly probably scanning for signs of the Ibex. Bove thought for a second, "Can you make it clearer?"

"No, this is the best I can do."

Bove studied the picture trying to distinguish any detail about the ship. It was difficult but slowly he began to make out its features, like front and back. Shortly he decided there was enough information for a plan which was already forming in his head.

"Okay," he said, "we are going to take out their engines."

"What?" Tom exclaimed, "You're going to get us killed!"

"Like I said, I'm getting us free from Zabi," Bove turned to Lucy. "Keep that image as clear as you can." Then to Jack, he said, "Plot us the shortest route to Ceti-3, then around to Ceti-2. Let them think we are going to Ceti-3."

"Will do," Jack responded.

"Dan, get ready to fire the rear blaster on my count."

"Are you sure?" Dan asked, "They have weapons. Better ones than us."

"Trust me."

"Jack, we're going to make a run for it so have the coordinates ready. Keep it steady, Lucy."

Bove fired the thrusters lightly turning the Ibex slowly, so the back was facing the back of the Dark Star. He adjusted its position based on the picture Lucy tried to hold steady on the main viewer. Little by little, he positioned the Ibex in a direct line with the Dark Star. He watched as the Dark Star rotated gaging when it would present its back to the Ibex. Slowly he fired the side thrusters to move the Ibex out from behind the asteroid so they would clear the asteroid when the back of the Dark Star faced them. He wanted it to look like they had drifted from cover.

"Okay," he said wiping sweaty palms on his pants, "Dan, on three, Jack on four, Lucy hold it."

He adjusted the Ibex slightly making sure it aligned directly to the Dark Star's engines. He fired the thrusters pushing the Ibex sideways into view of the Dark Star, then shut the thrusters down so they appeared to be drifting from behind the asteroid.

"Aw, there you are," Zabi said into the bridge of the Ibex, "Are you ready to give us our weapons? Or would you prefer to die?"

"We're ready," Bove said back switching off the radio, "One," a slight adjustment, "Two," another little movement, "Three."

Dan fired the blaster, Bove fired the thrusters, and turned to the right behind the asteroid just as another blast from the Dark Star missed the Ibex. The crew shifted to the left, but the restraining straps held them in place. Bove fired the main thrusters and Jack set course for Ceti-3 through the asteroid belt. Bove guided the Ibex missing rocks small as potatoes and others as large as buildings.

Again, the radio crackled and Zabi roared his anger at them, "You will pay for this. I guarantee it! There is no place you can hide. No place!" Bove switched the radio off.

"I don't want to hear that," he said to the crew.

"They are dead in space." Jack's face split into a huge smile.

"Yeah!" Tom roared.

Way to go!" Lucy said grinning at Bove.

"Damn!" Dan exclaimed.

"Get us to Ceti-2 as quick as you can," Bove let out a huge sigh of relief and a smile cut across his face.

"Will do," Jack said. As the Ibex cleared the asteroid belt heading for Ceti-3.

Thirty-One

Two days later the Ibex was within range of Ceti-2, a blue ball reminiscence of Earth. Oceans covered over half the planet, vast continents with green patches of forest, rivers snaking to the oceans, and brown areas of prairie and desert filled in between. Clouds covered wide sections of both land and ocean.

During the travel time, Bove had discussed with Stella how to confirm her story. She told him the rebel forces called themselves The Liberation Army. Their objective was to free the people from Ceti-2's corrupt government. According to the rebellion's leaders, they were going to replace the existing power structure with a new declaration of rights and freedoms. The problem, according to Stella, was that the document gave those rights and freedoms to a single class of the populous, which happened to be the wealthiest.

The rebels didn't say that in their speeches to the people, only that the current government was restricting access to certain rights by increasing costs beyond the reach of the people. Stella claimed the costs had decreased over the last several years relative to the overall cost of living increases. The major issue was the cost of education because without education one could not earn a reasonable income.

She had provided a connection to the

government's archives so Bove could review the documents she spoke of. He read the Liberation Army's declaration of rights and freedoms, and as Stella had said, it clearly stated "…the opulent citizens of Ceti-2 are all entitled to the rights and freedoms stated as…" The declaration of the government had no restrictions on rights and freedoms and the government forces were fighting to preserve their way of life. After reading the documents Bove was convinced Stella was being truthful about the rebellion, and it had to be stopped.

Stella told Bove to approach the main docking station which was the largest in the security ring that circled the planet. It was easily identified, but it was on the night side of the planet, so Bove diverted their course to circle to the far side.

As the Ibex reached the night side big patches of city lights illuminated the coastal lands with smaller cities and towns lighting the interior of the continents. As they approached the northern hemisphere an announcement came through the communication panel.

"Identify yourself and state your business." Bove went over to the captain's chair as Stella watched him. He leaned over and pressed the transmit button on the communications panel.

"This is the Ibex and we come in peace as a neutral party," Bove looked up at Stella.

"You are approaching the sovereign space of Ceti-2. Proceed to station one for inspection," The voice cut off filling the bridge with silence.

"Station one huh," Bove mused, "Okay."

Stella bent toward Bove, "That's good. It's the main station. When we get there, request a priority clearance. Tell them you have sensitive information."

Bove looked up at her. "Priority clearance?"

"Yeah." She nodded.

Bove returned to the pilot's seat and guided the Ibex toward the security ring. Station One was clearly visible and he could see docks for six ships. Other ships occupied three of the bays. In bay two lights flashed directing the Ibex to use that docking port.

Bove steered the Ibex toward bay two, slowing as they approached.

"Hold off docking," Stella said. "Ask for a priority clearance."

"Are we okay?" Bove turned to her.

"Just ask."

"Switch to transmit," Bove stood up stepped to the captain's chair and spoke into the communication panel. "I'm requesting a priority clearance. I have sensitive information."

"Complete the docking procedure and prepare for inspection." Came the reply.

Stella stood up, her face white with fear, "Get us out of here!"

Bove looked confused, turned back toward the main viewer, then back again to Stella. "Go!" she raised her voice.

"Dock and open your airlock." The voice was stern and demanding.

Bove pushed the transmit button on the console. "One moment." He said, "we are having a little problem with our alignment." He turned to Stella pressing the mute button.

"A priority clearance should have been acknowledged immediately. And with sensitive information, they would ask for verification. Stella was pale. "Someone would have been notified for verification."

Bove looked at her, confusion covering his face. "What?" he said.

"Get..us..out..of..here" Stella said punctuating each word.

Bove dropped into his chair and checked the docking bay. *Oh boy*, he thought. *This is going to be trouble.* He fired the reverse thrusters pushing the Ibex away from the docking station. The Ibex slowly backed out of docking bay two.

"You have violated the inspection protocol for entry into the Ceti-2 space and are now under arrest. Surrender or be fired upon."

Stella reached over and switched off the radio.

"What are you saying?" Bove asked her while turning the Ibex away from the station and firing the main thrusters.

"They're not following standard procedures. Someone should have been notified of the request. But it didn't happen, which tells me the rebels are in control of the security ring. If they find our cargo, we're as good as dead."

"Are you sure?"

"Yeah, I'm sure."

A laser blast hit the Ibex on the side causing the ship to veer to the right. Bove adjusted the course and started evasive moves checking the ship in pursuit. It fired again missing by a thread. Bove adjusted again, "Where to?" He asked Stella.

"Head for the far side in the southern hemisphere. With luck, we'll reach friendly air space once we cross to the south."

"Let's hope," Tom stared at Stella.

Bove kept evading laser shots from the pursuing ship. With no weapons to fight back their only hope was dodging the pursuer. They kept up the cat and mouse game until he crossed into the southern hemisphere at which point the rebel ship broke off and headed back up to the security ring. And immediately a ship approached from the surface and hailed them.

"State your name, affiliation, and business, or be fired on."

"Friendly," Stella cut in. "I'm Stella Thorne and we have weapons."

Another ship approached behind them and a third came to their side flying in tandem.

"Send your identification."

"Sure," Then to Bove she said. "Send my picture and a picture of this." She rolled up her sleeve and revealed a bar code tattooed on her forearm. She held her arm up for an image to be sent. Once the information was sent, she asked, "Satisfied?"

"Who's your crew?"

"They're friendly, harmless. They helped me."

"Follow us to the surface, and no tricks. Understood?"

"Understood," Bove said. Stella relayed that.

They followed the three ships to the surface and settled onto a landing pad. The other ships set down next to them. A team of soldiers surrounded the Ibex, and they were told to disembark. Bove opened the side crew door and lowered the entry steps, then stepped onto the top of the stairs looking out at the soldiers waiting for their exit.

"Come on," Stella stepped around Bove and started down the stairs. "They know who I am."

Bove followed descending to the landing platform followed by Jack, Lucy, Dan, and Tom. They stopped behind Stella when she halted a few feet in front of the soldiers. One of high rank stepped forward. "Greetings, your eminence," he said. "Your identity has been confirmed. Welcome back."

"Thank you." Stella waved her arm towards the Ibex, palm flat, "I bring a gift of weapons."

"Weapons?" The soldier asked.

"Yes," Stella looked over her shoulder at Bove. "They saved my life and secured the weapons."

"Very good." The soldier bowed to Stella.

She turned to Bove and nodded to the crew.

What the hell? Bove thought. *Your eminence, who the hell did we save. A royalty? Or someone as important?* he wondered.

"Do they have access to the hold to get the weapons?" Stella asked looking at Bove, then Tom.

Bove nodded. "I can give them access…."

"Do it," Stella interrupted.

Yeah, why would I not? Bove thought, then to Stella asked. "Who are you?"

"Does it matter?" she said. "You need to get the weapons unloaded quickly."

"Dan," Bove said, "get the loading bay opened and give them any help they need." Then he turned back to Stella, "Who are you?"

"I am Stella Thorne," she said.

"And who is that?"

"That's me." She flipped her hair behind her ear and gave Bove a sly smile.

"And just where do you fit in on this planet?"

"Well," Stella said, "I'm the daughter of Knar and Isia."

"Yeah, and who are they?"

"You don't need to know. Just accept that you're safe and when the weapons are unloaded, be on your way." She turned and started to the entrance at the end of the landing platform.

"Wait," Bove said stepping toward her.

"Leave. That's the best thing you can do." She said over her shoulder and stepped through the doorway.

Bove stared at the closed door wondering what just happened. "Yeah," he yelled, "with the rebels guarding the security ring, how are we supposed to get out of the system?"

"Fly off the south pole," One of the guards said standing next to him. "That's where the least resistance is."

"Yeah, okay." Bove looked at him. "Who is she?"

"She is Stella Thorne. The guard turned back to the unloading.

Heading back to the Ibex Bove wondered, *who did I just rescue?* Then he stepped on the loading ramp to the Ibex.

"Heads up," Tom called as Bove noticed a lift hauling crates down the loading ramp. He stepped aside to let them pass then continued up into the Ibex cargo bay where he found Tom watching the unloading of the weapons.

There were lifters lined up at the Ibex's loading ramp as one descended with a load of crates another entered for the next load. It made the process efficient; they knew what they were doing.

"How long till they're done?" Bove asked.

"Another hour," Tom answered.

Bove took the lift to the bridge and settled in his chair. *Okay*, he thought, *let's get out of here and out of this system, then we can figure out where we are, and what we want to do next. But first, we need to be away from here.*

He pressed the intercom button, "Lucy and Jack report to the bridge." A couple of minutes later Lucy and Jack arrived.

"Let's finish the transit set up so we can get out of this system quickly,"

"That's good with me," Jack said.

"Me too," Lucy added and sat facing her console, already working on the transit settings.

An hour later Tom announced over the intercom that the weapons were unloaded, and the cargo bay was secure. They were cleared to leave.

Is everyone on board? Bove wondered as he switched on the intercom.

"Everyone report your location and prepare for departure." Bove clicked off the intercom and fastened his security belt."

"I'm on my way to the bridge," Dan responded.

"I'm in the cargo bay and on my way up," Tom said.

Jack turned in his seat. "I'm here," he said.

Dan and Tom entered the bridge and settled into their seats.

"Let's get out of here," Bove said once everyone was secure. He fired the engines and headed towards the south.

"I hope the way's clear," Jack said.

There was no trouble getting off Ceti-2 and heading out of the system. Soon they were clear of the planet and well into open space.

"Now," Bove turned to the crew. "We have some decisions to make." He looked at each of them. They looked back, questions flitting across their faces and worry in their eyes.

"This ship belonged to Lucus, and you were his crew. Since his untimely death you have been following my lead, but now is the time to decide if you want me to stay, or you want to command the ship on your own. I know I'm new to the crew as the pilot and I've taken a leadership role, but that does not mean that I have to stay in that position, so you, all of you, have to make a decision as to how the control of the ship will be handled going forward."

"I think we need to get out of this system first," Jack said.

"I second that." Tom added, "Zabi will be looking for us."

"Yeah, the sooner the better," Lucy stated.

Dan nodded in agreement.

"Okay," Bove said. "But remember this conversation, there're still decisions to be made." He looked at each member of the crew as they turned to their tasks of finishing the transit setup. He turned to his console and began setting his controls still wondering if the crew would want to take the ship and continue their former activities.

"Ready for transit," Lucy stated.

Bove nodded to Lucy, then checked with Jack.

"Two minutes," Jack said." Where are we going?"

"Home," Bove said. "Home to the Sol system."

"Really?" Tom asked no one.

"Prepare to transit," Bove said.

"Well in answer to your question," Tom said. "We've stayed with you in hopes of a reward, but I have yet to see any credits coming our way. You know I'm in this for the credits and if there's nothing coming,

I vote to take the ship for ourselves and deliver the cargo where it belongs, that way we'll at least get a little compensation. And like you said you're new and really haven't earned a share of our cargo."

Jack and Lucy both turned to Tom questions flooding their faces.

"We have enough cargo to give us each five thousand credits," Tom added. "That's more than you'll get going back to Sol."

Jack and Lucy nodded and looked at Bove.

"Well," Dan said. "That is something to consider."

Lucy slowly nodded.

"You think the cargo's worth five grand?" Dan estimated.

"Yeah," Tom agreed. "I'm the one that knows what we have and where to sell it. So, yeah, it's worth five grand."

"That's over a thousand credits each," Dan said.

"Twelve hundred and fifty." Lucy put in.

"Okay," Bove held up his hands. "If you want to take the ship I understand. Can I at least request to be dropped on Earth?"

"Sure," Tom said standing up from his console and looking at Jack and Lucy. "You can be dropped anywhere you like."

Jack turned to Bove worry flooding his face, "Is that what you want?" he asked.

"Are we ready to transit?" Bove asked.

"Almost," Jack said.

"I'm ready," Lucy added.

A beep sounded from the command console. Bove looked toward it, as did the rest of the crew. Tom stepped to the captain's chair, pressed a button, and looked at the crew.

"Incoming message." The audio system announced. "For the safe return of Stella Thorne and the delivery of weapons that will aid in turning the tide of the rebellion, the citizens of Ceti-2 thank you. As compensation for your efforts, a deposit of 100,000 credits has been entered into each of your accounts. Once again thank you for your efforts." The channel went silent.

"Excellent!" Bove said.

"Wow!" Jack agreed.

"Wonderful!" Lucy cried.

"Terrific," Dan exclaimed.

Tom said, "Excellent indeed."

"Yeah!" Lucy yelled.

"Prepare to transit," Bove said as he executed the transit command.

The ship appeared in the Sol system, and everyone was quickly back to normal.

Tom looked at Bove, "What the hell, a hundred K?"

"Yeah, for services rendered," Bove said. "What'd you think? Not bad huh?"

"Not bad, it's phenomenal, unbelievable, more than I ever thought possible," Tom exclaimed. "Can you do that again?"

"Who knows," Bove said. "We do what we have to, and it goes from there."

"And," Jack looked around. "We'll do what we have to with Bove."

"Yeah," Lucy agreed. "This is the most we've ever gotten for a mission. You stay."

"Wait a minute," Bove said, "you said you wanted the ship, and you could deliver the cargo for a profit. What changed your mind?"

"Credits," Tom said. "Lucus never delivered a payday like this, and if you can do it once, you can do it again."

"I don't know." Bove started but was interrupted before he could finish.

"Doesn't matter," Jack said. "You did it once and you can do it again. We have faith in you."

"Lucy, Tom, Dan, you want me to stay?" Bove asked.

They all nodded. "Yeah," Tom said. "A hundred thousand credits, that's more than I got from Lucus in all the time I was with him, so yeah you can stay." Tom stepped back from the captain's seat. "And I guess this is yours." He waved a hand toward the chair with a slight bow.

"Okay," Bove said. "But now I have to pilot the ship." He leaned back in his seat in thought, then sat up. "Okay. First, we must improve this ship. We need weapons that can protect us and a transit drive that doesn't take all day to set up. Where can we get these?"

"Well." Dan turned his chair to face Bove. "I know a guy."

I can't remember anything I forgot

Made in the USA
Columbia, SC
10 February 2024

31228339R00162